DEVIL DOG

OUT OF THE DARK

BOYD CRAVEN

Copyright © 2016 Boyd Craven III

Devil Dog
By Boyd Craven

All rights reserved

Many thanks to Jenn for helping me tweak my cover to perfection!

Edited by Katy Light

Mailing list signup for new releases: http://eepurl.com/bghQb1

TABLE OF CONTENTS

CHAPTER 1

I was checking the traps in and around the tunnel. I wasn't hopeful that there'd be anything in them; we'd long since hunted and trapped out the area. Despite that, Chicago still had some semblances of life. Some of it was brutal, some of it so horror-stricken from the fires, the flames, and the ugly side of humanity… and then there was beauty. Friends, neighbors. Loved ones. Pulling together to try to overcome a tragedy so vast and so complete, I doubted that the country could survive and become again what it once was.

As if that would be much more of an improvement on now. The rumors I'd heard were that we'd been hit with an EMP. Terrific. Great. I knew what that meant.

A total reset.

Still, I had a job to do and responsibilities. No time for dicking around. Oorah.

See, most people will never understand what real hunger is until the trucks quit running and the trains stop dead... Suddenly, you're stuck in the middle of a large city. The first week, supplies were running low and the water stopped flowing for everyone. Sickness, hunger, and people settling old scores was horrible. After two weeks, people were living out of their pantries, except those who'd tried to leave the city on foot. By the third week, people were dying off due to a lack of medication and no air conditioning, in the middle of one of the hottest summers on record. Then, things got even worse.

"Let me go!" A woman's hoarse shout alerted me.

I lowered my pack to the ground, pushing it under debris, and made sure I still had the shotgun strapped tight to my back. I hadn't planned on leaving the tunnel today, but someone on the street above me had forced my hand.

"Mommy, they've got—" A young girl's voice cut off abruptly, and several angry voices shouted and threatened.

Chicago has a network of tunnels, some as close as right under the pavement. I've been living inside of them for almost three years now, when I'd cut myself off from society. I was at the edge of one of these tunnels, right by the gap between the road and a building where I could gain access to the topside. It wasn't my favorite place to come up, but I'd do it. I ran and leaped for the lip between the gap and caught it with my fingertips. The cold concrete crumbled, but my gloved fingers seemed to dig in, and I gained enough clearance to get an arm on the other side of the ledge and swing a leg up.

After that, it was easy to scramble over the concrete wall like a demented monkey on crack. The shouts had become quieter and I tried to pinpoint the sound. A motor fired up a moment later and drove off.

"Shit," I murmured, "I wish..."

If wishes were food, we'd all have full bellies. As it was, I'd need to move fast or risk someone targeting me, trying to rob me. Hell, even having a shotgun wasn't a deterrent. A shotgun with a full load out like I had was worth any ten lives to the slavers. In the home of the 44th president, there were few guns legally owned by citizens. When the fall happened, when the power went out for good, those who survived the fires that started near O'Hare, the folks with the illegal guns, came out to play. It wasn't pleasant. With no rule of law, the worst of humanity showed itself for what it really was.

I started walking, using the shadows to cover me, and I darted from cover to cover until I got past the entrance to our secret home. Time passed and I covered a lot of distance. Still, even with no one on the street, that didn't mean that I wasn't being watched from windows or rooftops. The smell of death, fire, and shit filled the city, almost gagging me. Even when I'd broken into an old sewer tunnel, it had smelled better than topside. I'd have to remember that the next time the little ones wanted to come up. Remind them how much better they had it.

Without conscious thought, my feet led me towards the intersection that some of the city's more upstanding citizens had started. Everyone there was armed with something, and it had become a place of barter and trade. You could find almost anything for sale, and the reason people even went out there was because it was as safe there as anyplace else. At least there, everyone was armed and not wanting to pick a fight or put up with bullshit.

I could smell fire, not the gasoline/diesel/plastic/death smell, but a wood fire and rounding the block, I stepped out of the shadows and walked towards the intersection where some cars had been pushed nose to end to form a walled off square, two cars deep. The one entrance, that doubled as an exit, was about three feet wide, with a gap in a corner where two vehicles hadn't been pushed tight together. It was, as always, guarded.

"Hey, Dickhead! You here to trade, my man?" Luis asked. He was a man I'd come to know over the course of the summer.

"Maybe. Who's got antibiotics today?" I asked him, already pretty sure where I'd end up.

If you want to know who's got what, and for the best price, ask the man who watches everyone go in and out. He was the new form of news, gossip and something the kids told me was called Craigslist. I don't know who the fuck Craig was, or why he had a list, but who cares. I can usually find anything here.

"Salina," Luis told me, "She's looking for meat or ammunition today. Or you could talk to Johnathon. He's got a collection of pills, but I think his prices are too high."

"Do you know what kind of pills?" I asked, my voice going hoarse. "Painkillers?" I hated the hopeful note in my voice.

"Shit, man," Luis spat, "You got off that junk. Nobody here's gonna sell you that shit. Your runner maybe, but no. No, Salina said—"

"Sorry," I said, wiping my lips, "It's… It's almost a habit, more than addiction," I said trying to make light of it, "Besides, I need the antibiotics. Mouse is sick."

Luis dropped a hand on my shoulder, giving it a friendly squeeze, "Get your antibiotics for the girl. What you're doing, man… I don't agree with the whole situation, but you're doing a good thing."

"Fuck doing a good thing," I said softly, "I'm doing what you guys should have done."

Luis looked perturbed, but he gave me a nod, stepped aside, and I walked into the small area. He knew I was right, but I'd paid the price for living life on my terms. I'd become a hunted man after the power went out for the topsiders, and now that there was no rule of law, there were certain people who would gladly pay ten women for my head if you believed the latest bounty rumors. Even though I was in a world full of trouble, I was allowed to come here. I'd gone to bat for a lot of these people. Some considered me a rabid animal, but one that wasn't aimed their way. Maybe it let them sleep at night.

* * *

The interior of the intersection had been cleared out to make space. Some people had permanent spots they liked to set up in and in the dusk, many of them were back-lit by barrels with some sort of wood burning in them, and most of them had large pots simmering stews and soups of sorts. For people who didn't want a permanent spot, they came in, laid down a blanket or sheet, and sat on it. They would put their wares out and sit until someone would come walking by. Money was worthless unless it was old silver coins. Nickels, quarters, dimes. Sometimes real silver or gold bullion showed up, but the real treasures were ammunition, medicines, and things that used to be so mundane. But they made living in this post-apocalyptic world possible again.

A Coleman camp stove was for sale at one spot I walked by, and a man was holding up two rats, insisting that the vendor was getting the better end of the deal. I smirked; he didn't know what he was talking about. That camp stove was worth six tunnel rats, not two. The man became loud and two other vendors slowly pulled their guns and knives, in case violence started. I sidestepped and went the other way, looking for Salina, as some of the wandering guards came over to check things out.

I passed quite a few people who had food openly out there for sale. Bread, baked somewhere in a secret location. Some of it was made with standard yeast, but more and more sourdough was being used. I didn't know where the grain or flour was being purchased from but knew there had to be a store of it somewhere. I almost drooled as I thought about having a slice of hot bread with some butter slathered over the top of it. Looking away from the bread was almost as hard as not thinking about the pain pills.

Which, of course, got me thinking about the pills again. Two sullen looking teens darted in front of me, almost tripping me. I put out a hand and snagged one of them on impulse.

"Hey, man, be cool," the young man said.

"Hey, there was a snatch and grab over my way. You know who's operating there now?"

The kid looked at me, recognition making his eyes open wide.

"Dude, I don't know anything," he said.

I fished in my pocket and pulled out two .22lr shells. The skinny boy licked his lips. It wasn't enough to get him a full meal, but it was more than enough to get a bowl of greasy stew that was forever being added to. The never-ending soup.

"How about now?" I asked, letting go of him and pressing them into his hand.

"You're putting me in a tough spot here," the young man said, looking to his friend that had stopped with him.

"Who'd they snatch?" His friend said in a feminine voice.

I was almost startled and looked closer. I had thought that the two were both young men, but on closer inspection, I could make out the delicate bone structure and facial features behind the dirt and grime that was artfully placed. The young woman's hair had been hacked off roughly. The clothing she wore was baggy, but she was so gaunt that if she was trying to hide curves, there wasn't much left of them. Hunger did that to people.

"A mother and daughter, I think. They were fast. I couldn't get a look at them. They had a working car or truck."

"I don't want to get involved, man," the young man said, handing me the shells back. "I can't. My wife…"

I looked at the both of them. They looked as if they were three meals away from starvation. I took the man's hand in my left and pressed the shells back into it and closed his fingers over into a fist.

"I... family is important," I told him.

His mouth dropped open in shock.

"Is your name really Dickhead?" The woman asked, surprising her husband.

"It's what you topsiders call me," I admitted.

"I think you're like a big, old, mean junkyard dog," she said, a smile tugging at the corner of her lips, "There to protect people, but at heart, you're not so mean."

"Don't let that shit get out," I snarled, "I don't want every beggar and idiot expecting handouts from me. I just…"

The woman reached out, took my hand and gave it a squeeze. "I promise. Nobody will know that the Dickhead Devil dog is a good guy." The man gaped, looking between her and me, and I realized that people around us had gone silent.

"Get the fuck out of here, if you're not going to help," I said loudly, giving the young man a shove.

The woman got it. She dropped me a wink and pulled him away. Nobody wanted to be caught giving me the information on where the slavers operated. The price on me was too big. They would cut down anybody to get to me. I'd been loud and shoved him at the end because people had noticed that I'd been taking the time to talk to them and I'd offered payment. By shoving him and yelling, I was just another asshole trying to shakedown the young couple.

"Making friends, I see," a silky voice said.

I turned, and Salina was there in front of me. Her ebony skin gleamed, despite the darkness. She was a stunning beauty. More important than her physical looks, were her abilities as a doctor and healer. You would think that she'd give away her services for free, but she didn't. She did, however, trade reasonably, and her medicines were life savers.

"Salina," I said, pulling her close to hug her, "I need a favor," I whispered in her ear, the hug meant to cover my question.

"Come. Jerome is at my table. Let's talk there, where we can trade." Her voice had a Caribbean lilt that had broken the hearts of many men.

As beautiful as I found her, I'd never been enthralled with her the way most men here were. A few shot me jealous looks at the hug and the seemingly casual familiarity that I had with her. Doctor

Salina had run the North Side Clinic, and I'd used her for years. A homeless veteran didn't have much choice and the VA was useless. She'd gotten me off the junk twice now. After the second time, she forbade people from selling anything narcotic to me, threatening them with refusing to treat them later in life. I was finally able not to be angry about that, as selfish as it seemed.

"Yeah," I said hoarsely, "Mouse is sick."

"You should let the girl and her brother come up with us. I will protect her," she said without looking at me.

I followed her to her table. Her eldest son, Jerome, stood behind it. He was almost six and a half feet of solid muscle and he looked to be twenty seconds away from violence at any given moment. The truth was, he was a little slow, but a good kid. Almost twenty years old. In the ordinary course of life, he'd have made a good general laborer… but his mental deficiencies matched mine. His brain didn't retain much, whereas mine slipped from time to time.

"She won't leave Pauly and he won't come topside willingly," I told her.

"Well then, let's see what we can do." She walked behind her little table, spoke into Jerome's ear and he smiled and settled into a sitting position against one of the cars used as a backdrop. "What's her symptoms?" she asked.

"Trouble breathing. Her breath sounds soupy and she's running a fever. Lots of discharge from her nose, and when she coughs. I've got her separated from the group for now, but I… She's not allergic to anything I know of and…"

"You don't want her to infect the others, but you're worried enough to come topside for pills, instead of one of your crazy capers."

"I'm not crazy!" I snarled, regretting the words immediately.

Jerome stood in a hurry, looming over the three-foot table that separated us. He didn't scare me, but he didn't know that.

"I didn't say you were, Richard," she said softly, too softly for the crowd that had started forming up around us to hear.

"I can't… She's only six," I told her. "What do you have?" I asked.

She had various metal containers set out on the table, some of them old army ammunition storage boxes. In one, she dug around and pulled out a large white bottle. She counted out pills in her hand and dumped them into a plain white envelope.

"Twice a day for ten days. If the fever doesn't break in three days, come back here. You have Tylenol? Motrin? Something safe for her to take?"

I nodded, but they had done nothing. I told her that.

"That's probably because it's something like pneumonia or a severe respiratory infection. The child really needs to move topside. Those dank, dark tunnels…"

"Doc," I told Salina, "we've had this talk. Both the girl and the boy were used. Badly. She'd go into hysterics if any man other than the boys in the group or I got near her. Pauly is so scared, he's never going to go for it. I just need to get her healthy for now."

"I know… You do what you can."

"How much?" I asked her.

"Four twelve gauge shells. Buckshot."

I snorted.

"I need the pills… but, *four shells*?" I asked her, almost hoping she was joking.

"No joke. I gave you some Clindamycin. Some of the strongest stuff I have. Mouse didn't kick whatever crud she had the last time. If it were something lightweight like Keflex, it'd be cheaper, but I don't think it'd work. You do want this to work, Dickhead? Don't you?" Her words at the end rose in volume.

I suddenly wasn't the center of attention, just another guy haggling for goods and services.

"Yeah, ok," I said, hating to have to pay that much.

I was prepared to give up a pocketful of loose mismatched ammo, or even some meat if my traps had caught anything. As it was, I did have enough shells, but I used buckshot almost exclusively. I dug three shells out of my pocket and set them on the table.

"You're still one short," she said, tapping the table next to the envelope for emphasis.

"Dammit, we're friends. Isn't three enough?" I asked.

"We are not friends. You are an asshole, if anything. I'm already giving you a deal. I would usually ask for five shells, *and* a dog."

I paused to consider it and then shrugged. I pulled the Keltec KSG to the front of me. It was a drop-sling, which allowed me to carry it a number of different ways. I racked the slide and ejected a pair of shells. I put one brass side first on the table, a little harder than I'd intended. The second one went into my pocket.

"Here you go," she said, sliding the envelope towards me.

I let the shotgun drop down on the sling to free up my hands, and I folded the envelope carefully and tucked it into my pocket.

"Thanks," I told her, "I… It's just that…"

"There's no apologies needed. You've always been difficult. A good man, but difficult. Rough around the edges. My Jerry would have loved to have had you as a friend."

That hurt. Her husband had been one of Chicago's finest. Gunned down at a traffic stop. Salina's office had been peppered with pictures of him, a reminder of what she'd lost, way back before the lights had gone out. Now, she had her son and a weird sort of lifestyle going on. It worked for her, just like my subterranean existence worked for me.

"Doc, my arm…" a man said, pain filling his voice.

I stepped back and a man with an apparently broken arm was approaching. Jerome was already getting a folding chair out for the man while Salina got a bag out from behind them.

"Tell that precious girl and boy that they are

welcome to come with me. I'll give them a home," she told me and made a shooing gesture with one hand.

"I'll pass it along. Again."

I turned and headed back toward the exit. More and more lately, it seemed that people were coming here. It was a safe space. A place where they could find their essentials without worrying too much about being preyed upon by the roving gangs that had taken over parts of the city. Carving out their own fiefdoms. Luis was talking with some new folks and I had to wait for them to finish, so I could squeeze out. He saw me and held up a hand, motioning for me to wait. I did and he pointed out who had some tools for sale to the new guys. When he was done, I stepped through.

"Hold up," Luis's voice was loud. Commanding.

I turned to see him red in the face.

"If I hear of you harassing anybody in here again, I'm going to throw your ass out!" He was all but screaming.

It was one of probably a dozen outbursts like this he had to make in a day I was sure, but I hadn't…

When he grabbed me, his left hand worked its way under the sling for the shotgun. My first instinct was to have broken his grip, then his wrists, but it was Luis and he was one of the good guys. I felt something lodge under the sling, and he pushed me back.

"Sorry, man. Won't happen again," I said confused.

"Make sure it doesn't."

“It was a misunderstanding,” I told him though I was the one who didn’t know what the hell was going on.

“Then get the hell out of here.”

I left and when I was ten feet away, I pulled out a small piece of cardboard he’d tucked under the sling. ‘4th and Elms’, the slip said. I smiled. The girl from earlier or her husband had slipped this to Luis.

“Oh, what a tangled web we weave, when first we practice to deceive,” I muttered to myself and hurried west, instead of towards the nearest entrance to my home.

CHAPTER 2

It didn't take me long to figure out where the hastily scratched note had led me to. I could hear the party going on long before I could see it. Half a dozen men were shouting, laughing and passing bottles of dark amber booze around, and the other half were just standing or sitting on the concrete, taking their turns with the bottle. Probably whiskey, bourbon or... I shook my head. I couldn't allow myself to obsess over the booze, just like I couldn't obsess over the pills, or the crank or the...

Instead, I focused on where they were at, from a safe distance. I used my binoculars to figure things out.

An old Ford pickup truck was parked in front of a small branch bank. On the sidewalk out front, a barrel was lit, and the fire made the light around the laughing figures dance. They were having a party. I recognized one of them, a white hood rat I'd let live the last time he'd taken up with some bad dudes. I'd given him a shot, but apparently he'd taken up with some new losers. His loss. Literally it would cost him his life someday. He looked down and jerked his foot, and that's when I saw them.

The woman was my age, maybe a little younger. Early forties. The form next to her could have been a teen or a young woman, it was hard to tell. Both had their wrists and ankles zip tied together. They'd been laying down flat on the ground and with the coming darkness, I'd missed seeing them. I considered the range, and even thought about reloading the KSG with slugs, but the distance was too great.

I'd have to move in closer. Once they sold the women, it would be almost impossible to save them. The only way I'd been able to make a difference before, was catching them when it was just the small gangs like this. Hopefully, the worst hadn't happened to them yet. See, that's the other thing that had surprised the hell out of me, even though I'd seen it happen in other countries. Women and children suddenly became property or play toys for the sick games played by twisted people who didn't have to worry about the cops anymore.

The shithead I'd let go before was named Curt or Curtis. He knelt down and grabbed the wrists of the women, jerking them both to their feet roughly, and called out to someone. Another man took a hard swallow on a bottle of booze and walked over, looking the women over from head to toe. A second man joined him. I was not about to watch these women be raped right in front of me, so I started moving quickly in the shadows, closing the distance.

I stopped when, instead of pushing them towards the building, the men pushed them towards the pickup truck. Curtis stopped, cupping a hand on the woman's stomach, and moving it up to cop a feel. I was sickened by the fucker and vowed he'd die. It was worse than mugging people for a can of food. He'd gone beyond the pale in my opinion.

The raven-haired woman spat at him, jerking her head back. She hit Curtis in the nose with a double fist, and he shoved her forward, almost bending her in half as her stomach hit the tailgate. With one hand cupping his nose, he used his free hand to push her into the bed of the truck. One of the men crawled back there with her, a long gun resting securely in his hands. I could hear the jeers and wolf-whistles from the other men - and then I got a good look at the younger lady.

I knew how old she was. She was fourteen, going on fifteen. I'd seen that face after every deployment, and although she'd grown while I was off fighting in a war somewhere, I'd have recognized her anywhere. Maggie, my daughter. I almost broke into a run. I'd been certain she was gone, long gone away in Arkansas with her mother and grandparents. Why was she here?

I was sickened as one of the three men came up behind her, pulling his body close to her backside and started feeling the curves of her body. My blood boiled, but like the woman she'd been traveling with, she tried to fight back. This guy was a lot faster than Curtis and laughed as he ducked back. Then, he scooped her up and put her in the bed of the truck, closing the tailgate. She spat at him, and he slugged her in the face. She fell backward, out of sight, and he climbed in and held the gun out towards the raven-haired woman.

"I'm going to fucking kill you, too," I cussed, moving faster.

I had already done a mental tally; there were a dozen people in plain view. All were armed, as far as I could tell. As it was just me, I knew had to plan this carefully and pray that my daughter wasn't seriously hurt. But I had to stop that truck before it got out of sight. The third man got into the driver's seat. After shaking a handkerchief out of his pocket and holding it to his nose, Curtis got into the passenger seat. The truck fired up, and the headlights cut through the darkness.

"Oh, shit," I said to myself and slid into an alleyway between two stalled cars.

The motor noise rose as they gave it gas and then the tires slipped as the genius working the clutch gave the old stick shift truck too much gas. They'd probably stolen the truck, probably had never driven a stick before. Still, an old vehicle that worked was priceless, as most of them had been commandeered by people who'd claimed to be law enforcement a month back. I shrank into the shadows as the truck shot past. I hurried now and broke into a dead run, my heart laboring with the possibility that I didn't have enough time to stop them before I lost Maggie…

The truck slowed down at an intersection where the cars that had stalled during the EMP had been abandoned. I heard the motor cut out after the truck lurched sickeningly. They'd stalled it. I heard the faintest of laughs and jeers from the group behind me, having fun at their expense. It was almost lost to the sound of my boots slapping the pavement. I was so close…

The truck fired up again, and I pulled out my target pistol, a small Beretta .22 and started firing. Sparks flew up from the pavement, and the rear tire blew out just as the men got the truck moving. The four shots I'd taken sounded sharp, and I would have to move fast. They had to have heard it, as evidenced by the wide-eyed look of the man in the back of the truck. He started swinging his gun out behind him, taking his eyes off the raven-haired woman. I holstered the .22 and ran harder.

Time, space and distance seemed to slow, and I knew I was getting tunnel vision. My entire focus was the back of the truck. I was aware of the shouts behind me, but they were too far away, I had too much of a head start. If I was quick and clever, I had a good couple minutes before they realized that I had been the shooter and not them. It was all I needed, along with a healthy dose of luck… Which was delivered by the raven-haired woman using both feet, ankles still zip-tied together, to kick the man in the bed right over the tailgate and onto the pavement.

I slowed enough to take a snapshot with the KSG. It had materialized in my hands without me even thinking; my old training was kicking in. The buckshot tore into the back of the man's neck and shoulder even as he was hitting the ground. The driver's side door opened, and the weasel-dicked motherfucker got out. He was already bringing to bear a pistol. I shot him in the chest as I ran closer.

"Curtis," I screamed, racking another shell.

The shouts I'd heard behind me had gotten louder, but they hadn't gotten any closer. I put a shot into the other rear tire as I skidded to a halt, ten feet behind the pickup's bed. A high feminine scream came from somewhere, the bed of the truck probably. I'd been careful with my shot, though, the rear tire blew out, and Curtis's bloody figure jerked to a stop. He'd been trying to slide from the passenger's side to the driver's side. I heard the starter on the truck kick in, it must have stalled it when I'd started shooting… so I started moving forward again, putting a shot into the front passenger side tire.

Five shots so far. I wasn't worried. I had enough left and with the tires being blown out, the truck stalled again as Curtis or Curt put his hands up. It barely lurched when it stalled, but he got out of the truck slowly.

"Curtis," I said looking into the bed of the truck. The woman had quit screaming but was sobbing uncontrollably, shaking my daughter.

"Don't… I… Oh shit. I promise, man, I promise..." I wasn't paying attention to his words so much as watching his hand that had snaked behind his back.

He pulled the revolver out, almost in slow motion, and my gun went off. Most of the pellets hit the gun and his hand, and he screamed as if I'd just doused him with fire. I chanced a look behind me, and in the now twilight, I could see figures running. None were in too good a shape by the looks of things, and many of them were huffing already. I had to move fast.

"How's Maggie?" I asked the raven-haired woman.

"What?" She asked, her sobs coming to a stop. She wiped her nose with her sleeve and looked at me, "They hit her, knocked her out. I hope she isn't..."

"Curtis. Where were you taking the women?" I asked him.

He just screamed and held out his hand. His thumb and first two fingers were mostly gone, his middle finger hanging on by a mangled thread. The ground was turning scarlet underneath him.

"Curtis, where were you taking my daughter?" I screamed at him.

I'd found her, she was safe for another ten seconds, but I wanted to know where the drop off point was. Where the main gang was hiding out.

"Fuuu... fuck... fuck you," He spat.

I shot him in the kneecap at close range and turned my back on him as he started screaming in agony. I let the shotgun drop, the sling taking its weight and letting it settle on the front of my chest. I reached in and scooped up Maggie, pulling her from the screaming woman's arms.

"Don't," I yelled at her, "We need to leave now. They're coming."

"What are you doing?" she sobbed, but she started moving.

I readjusted Maggie to hang halfway over my shoulder, the one that didn't have the shotgun and pulled out a knife I had clipped in my pocket, flicking it open. The woman flinched backwards.

"You can't run if you're still tied up. I don't have time. If you don't hurry your ass, I'm going to leave you here. I won't let them get my daughter."

The woman looked at me in horror, but shaking and crying, she moved towards the side. I sawed through the bindings on her wrists and handed her the knife. She cut her ankles free and handed the knife back to me. I folded it and stored it and held out a hand for her to hold onto. She climbed out of the truck, still crying, half in shock, half numb and wobbly on her feet.

"I need you to keep up with me," I told her, "If you can keep up with me, I promise you, I can get you away from these people."

"Please, don't hurt us," she begged, but she moved.

"I promise, I have no intention of hurting you," I told her, starting to move towards a darkened street.

* * *

The men had gotten to the truck about two minutes later than they should've. Apparently, they hadn't been on the same survival diet as everyone else. That, or they were poor physical specimens. The half mile jog had taken them too long. I watched them take in the carnage and look around right before I closed the back door to the old theater, being careful not to bang Maggie's head on the jam. I'd sent the woman ahead of me. I barred the door and walked slowly.

Maggie was breathing easier, and she was starting to move. Hopefully, the blow to the head hadn't given her a serious concussion. I didn't have much time to check now, but I knew she was alive. I could feel her chest contracting with every breath, her body warm against my shoulder and back.

"Are we safe here?" the woman asked, the tears drying up.

"No, this is a doorway," I told her.

"A doorway to where?" she asked, giving me a wide-eyed look.

"It's one of the ways down. I don't use this place much, but I think the noise above will have my people waiting. You'll be safe," I assured her and walked towards the back, snapping on a penlight with my free hand.

Behind the screen was a storage room. I pushed the door open and the woman followed me, closing it behind us. The room was full of cleaning materials and a hundred years of detritus. I walked towards the back and knelt down to pull a ring in the floor. The trapdoor went down.

"Oh, my God, we can't hide here," the woman said, "There're rats and..."

"This is just one way in," I told her. "We have to hurry."

The gangs had tried to burn me out of old buildings on more than one occasion. They didn't know that I knew the underground as well as anyone left alive could. I'd spent a couple of years working for the Chicago Transit Authority during my divorce. Underneath here was a way to the deeps, between forty and a hundred feet below the streets above.

"Oh God, what is that?" the woman asked, as my light hit a metal square door, hanging somewhat ajar. It had been rusting in place silently for over a century now.

"Coal chute," I told her, sweating heavily now. "Follow me."

Maggie's weight was starting to get to me. Lack of good food, lack of exercise and letting my PT go lax were the biggest causes of it, but now that the adrenaline was wearing off, I was feeling drained and weak. I gave the woman one last look, and she shuddered, but she wasn't looking at me. She was looking at the door.

"Is it... Will I fall?" she asked.

"No, it's like a slide. Use your feet to the sides as soon as you get in to slow yourself. I don't have a rope in this one. It's mostly a quick escape."

"An escape from what?" she asked me, the tears forming again.

Voices and a banging sound from somewhere nearby startled her, and I motioned her to go first.

"Them. I've got Maggie, you go. When you get down there, get out of the opening, so I don't bump into you. You'll be safe down there. My people are nearby."

"Did they go in here?" a loud voice yelled from somewhere else.

With a jolt, the woman went towards the opening. I gave her my penlight, and she crawled in. I hoped she didn't startle and scream when she felt how slick the chute was. She went in, her clothing making a soft whooshing sound as she disappeared. I pulled my daughter off my shoulder and felt her face in the darkness. I could feel a lump forming on her temple, and I only wished I could have hurt the man who'd punched her worse. All things considered, dead was dead, and Curtis had quit screaming half a minute ago.

I held her in front of me like a small child, like the last time I had held her before I'd deployed to Afghanistan, and before things had gone south with her mother, Mary. I crawled in, after waiting a moment, listening for the others, and then I went down. I used my boots against the sides of the wall to slow my descent. The chutes had been made to both haul coal and dispose of ash in the buildings they serviced. It kept the topside neat and clean, freed up traffic, and was a quick way to move supplies about the city, back in the day. Most of this was now forgotten, and it was my ticket out.

After what seemed like an eternity, I felt her stir and she whimpered.

"It hurts," she said.

"Shhhh," I told her. "It's ok, Maggie. I got you. I don't know how you got here, but I got you." She gasped and in the darkness, a foot lashed out, hitting me in a tender spot. I forgot about keeping my pace slow, and we slid down into the blackness at a breakneck speed. She struggled against me and I tried to keep her head down, so she wouldn't hit the roof of the chute. I felt it the moment I came off the end because I was airborne, falling the last six feet and landing hard on the dirt-packed ground. All the air was pushed out at once and my daughter pushed herself away from me. I rolled over, taking long breaths when my chest quit contracting, and then a pen light snapped on.

I was blinded and I held up a hand, so my eyes wouldn't burn out. I took a physical stock of things and decided I was bruised, but nothing was broken.

"Sir, thank you for rescuing us, but if you'd show me the way out, my daughter and I are leaving." The woman's voice was cold and clear.

"Hey, I'm not holding you here, but my daughter, Maggie stays. Mags, you doing ok, kid?"

"Who's Maggie?" I heard my daughter ask. I pulled myself up and felt around in my pants pocket and found a book of matches. I pulled one out and lit it with trembling hands.

The penlight quit shining in my eyes and in the softer glow of the match, stood the woman and... Oh, dammit. Not again. Not again. I slumped to the ground. Hot tears burned my cheeks.

"I'm sorry, I thought you were my daughter," I said, my chest starting to hitch despite my best efforts.

The match was starting to burn at my fingertips and I tossed it.

"Mom, let's go," the girl said, pulling on her arm.

"You thought she was your daughter?" the woman asked, looking startled.

"I… It's been some time. I thought… In the dark… I'm sorry if I scared you. I wasn't going to let those animals take you anyway, but I thought I'd found…"

Something invisible sucker-punched me in the gut, and a sob escaped me. The feeling of loss was like the day I'd been coming out of the hospital and I'd been sharing a room with Baker, the kid who'd stepped on a land mine. He'd died of his wounds weeks later from a complication in the surgery. I'd known that my wife had consulted a lawyer and I was being served with divorce papers. I'd loved the idea of being a father, but I'd never been around to actually try it out.

"Are you ok, mister?" the girl asked, taking a step forward, putting her hand on my arm.

In the semi-darkness, I used a sleeve to wipe my face, but her touch had a calming effect on me. I must have terrified them as much as the men topside had, maybe worse, because I'd killed the others to get to them. Still, my admission and breakdown must have calmed them.

"Yeah, I'm sorry. That must have scared you. I didn't mean to," I said simply.

"You got us away from those men," the woman said.

"I'm… Hell, topside, they call me Dickhead, but you can call me Dick," I told them and smiled when the young girl snickered, despite looking like she was going to barf all over me.

The woman stepped close and handed me the penlight. "I'm Jamie O'Sullivan, and this is my daughter Melanie, or Mel."

I stood slowly, and I seemed to be having a harder time than Mel, though she was the one who'd gotten the knock on the head, not I. I felt for the shotgun and turned towards the wall and pulled it up to inspect in the light. Thankfully, I hadn't landed on it, but I would take it apart and check it out when I got home.

"Nice to meet you. I can show you the way out, but I would advise you to lay low for at least a couple of days. I'm not well-liked and after killing three of them and snatching you too, they're likely to be out in force for a while." I told them.

"You said you have people down here," Jamie said, "Are they close by?"

"Yeah, just about everyone I have left in the world is about twenty minutes' walk away," I told her.

"Well, let's go," Mel said, "This place is creepy."

I heard something screech far above and I held my finger over my lips to shush them. From far above, light shone down, and then something started banging around inside the tunnel. I moved fast, using my arms to pull both ladies out of the way as a small trash can came tumbling into the weak light.

"I don't see nothing," a voice above yelled to someone, their words almost lost by the distance of forty feet.

I indicated a direction with a jerk of my head and the ladies nodded. We moved out slowly and I kept the penlight held down on a slight angle ahead of me, so the ladies could see where to place their feet. I'd stop once in a while at an intersection and look at the markings that led in different directions and briefly wondered about taking strangers into the home site, but I mentally shrugged and decided that if they remembered, they weren't a threat to me.

The pain of thinking I'd found Maggie and then realizing I'd done it again was agonizing. I knew Jeremy would have a small bout of laughter about it, maybe some of the others, but it hurt. Every time it happened, it hurt.

"Boss," a loud voice came out of the darkness.

"Jeremy," I said, hearing the oldest of the kids, "Those with great power," I said just as loud.

"Comes great responsibility," the voice said, and a light snapped on as we completed the hokey challenge that let him know I was safe and not under duress.

I was ready for the light, but the ladies gasped behind me as it flicked on and then flicked back off.

"Picking up strays again, boss?" Jeremy asked.

"Pulled them from Curt's boys," I told him.

"They hurt?"

In the darkness, I could hear him opening the door behind him and I clicked on the penlight again.

"Is that a bomb shelter?" Mel asked.

"No, it's a water hatch. A long time ago, these tunnels flooded."

"That's not safe," Jamie said.

"Oh no, ma'am, it's totally safe. The utilities run through here. Come on," Jeremy turned on his big halogen hand light again and stepped through.

"It's safe. Come on, I'll introduce you to the crew," I told them and stepped through the nearly four-foot hatch, that was set a foot off the ground.

They followed me in and the almost six-foot round tunnel turned a right-hand corner, and both me and Jeremy killed our lights. Kerosene and oil lamps lit the opening. Maggie, I mean, Mel gasped. A dozen kids of various ages came streaming up and I took off the shotgun sling, handing it to Jeremy as I got tackled. Three kids wrapped around my legs and the rest pushed me backwards until we all fell in a laughing heap.

"One, two, three. You're out, sucka!" a boy laughed loudly.

A sullen teenage girl stood by, twirling her hair and tried to look bored.

"Oh look, more mouths to feed," she quipped.

The kids scrambled off me, and more than one gave me a big squeeze and whispered that "they got me that time" before I could stand. Mel stood there, her mouth agape, but her mom had an amused grin on her face. I smiled back and shrugged my shoulders.

"Danielle, this is Jamie and Melanie," I said

pointing out the women. "This is Danielle, our resident sourpuss, diaper changer, and cook," I said, watching the teen turn a furious shade of red, and not from embarrassment.

"Dude, you're telling me, you found a baby?" Danielle said.

"No, but if I did, you'd totally be the one to change the diapers," I told her.

"In your dreams, grandpa," she said and stalked away.

"Are these all..." Melanie started to say, but her words ran out as she took in the scene.

The room served as a utility junction. The lower parts of the floor were wet and damp, but a three-foot raised platform had been built. Overall, the section we called home was close to thirty feet by forty feet. There was an even higher raised mezzanine of about twenty by twenty in one corner, and everyone's bedrolls and bedding stood there.

"Orphans. I'll introduce you to all of them, after tackling me, they got shy," I told them, watching as the younger ones ran back to a large open spot on the mez and sat down.

We'd done this before, and they were waiting for me to make introductions.

"I hear we're having meat tonight in the soup," Jeremy told me, clapping me on the shoulder, and he put my shotgun on my hammock that I kept by the mez and walked up, sitting amongst the younger kids.

"Do I want to know?" Mel asked.

"These are kids who have no one else left," I told

her, "I do what I can. I help whoever I can if..."

"Oh, who's that?" Jamie asked.

Standing almost four feet tall, Mouse came running from somewhere on the mez and when she leaped I caught her easily out of the air. The little girl buried her head in my neck and gave me a big squeeze before coughing and hacking. Her body was warm, warmer than it should have been. I slowly put her down on the edge of the mez.

"Easy, you aren't supposed to be up and out of bed," I told her.

"Uncle Dick, I missed you. You were gone for like... ten years."

I could see the fever in her, but she was smiling. She must be breathing easier still, I'd give her the pills. Actually, that'd be Danielle's job.

"Are these new friends? Are they going to stay?" she asked quickly.

"They're friends," I told her, "whether or not they stay is up to them. I'm going to introduce them to the group. You want to help me?" I asked her.

Mouse stood and held out her hand. I took it and she tugged on it, so I leaned down. Her voice was quiet and in a whisper.

"What's her name?" she asked pointing to Jamie.

"Jamie," I told her.

"Hey, everybody!" Mouse yelled and all of the chatter stopped, and all eyes turned to look at us. "Uncle Dick has some new friends for us," she said, coughing.

I smiled. The kid was sick, but she tried so hard

to be a grown up. She looked to be around six, but she wasn't sure, and her brother wasn't much help in figuring things out.

"This is Jamie," she said, pointing out the older woman, "And this is..."

"Maggie!" all the kids yelled as one voice.

My face turned scarlet and I let go of Mouse's hand and started walking. The tears flowed freely.

CHAPTER 3

"There you are," Danielle said, coming out of the darkness of the tunnel.

I hadn't gone far, but I needed time to get my shit together. Today was what I'd consider a bad day, but I'd imagine it was a bad day for more than one reason to most people.

"Hey," I told her.

She slid down next to me by the wall.

"You freaked out that lady a bit, taking off like that."

"I didn't mean too. I thought I'd found her. She's even the right age..."

"Hey," Danielle said, "They're ok. I explained things. When you get stressed, you kind of..."

"Go crazy?" I asked her. "I mean, Melanie doesn't look anything like Maggie."

"With what you've been through and how the Topsider gangs are hunting you, it's ok to be a little crazy. We all owe you our lives."

I think I almost choked. Danielle had not only insulted me, but she'd also complimented me in the same breath… and I felt the weight on my chest lifting.

"Now, I got one today, in one of the traps down by the park. It was feral, and there's enough meat for everyone to have two bowls of soup."

I smiled, "You and Jeremy keeping things held together when I melt down… I appreciate it," I told her, meaning every word of it.

"Sir, yes sir," she said with a mock salute, and I half sobbed, half laughed.

"Why are you suddenly so grown up?" I asked her.

She was silent and thought about it for a moment. Danielle had been one of the first kids I'd saved, and the gangs topside had been operating for a while now… so I got her early on. Still, she'd have both mental and physical scars from her ordeal.

"You never treated me like a kid. You always talked to me like a grown up. I guess…" She brushed a lock of hair out of her eyes, "I realized that arguing with you about everything was me being… well, I was a pain in the ass, but I think I was doing it because I thought that's what you expected of me. If that makes any sense at all."

I laughed loudly at that, "No, but teenagers never made sense to me. Come on, kid," I said, and I stood, offering her a hand.

"Did you tell Melanie and Jamie what the meat was?" I asked her.

"Oh, it was the lady, Jamie, who skinned it."

I stopped and looked at her, making sure she wasn't pulling a fast one on me. She wasn't.

"Really?"

"Really. Apparently her husband was some sort of crazy survivalist. I talked to her for a while..." Jamie looked away from me, "she reminds me of my mom, you know?"

"I never knew your mom," I said and pushed her, smiling as she stumbled a bit, "But I think she'd tell me what I already know."

"Oh yeah?" She arched an eyebrow.

"You're a good kid, and someday you and Jeremy will be—"

This time, I was the one who got shoved, it was more of a slow punch to the shoulder with a push, but I saw I'd hit a sensitive spot with my jibe. They'd been circling each other, sharing insults whenever they didn't think I was paying attention.

"That's not even funny," she said.

Yes, it was, but I wasn't going to make her misery worse and tell her that Mouse had already informed everyone, except Jeremy and Danielle, that she was going to be their flower girl. Of course, Mouse expected everything to happen down here, below ground. She carried mental scars almost as dark and deep as I did.

"That was a little bit funny. Let's eat."

* * *

"So how long have you been down here?" Mel asked me, while Pauly, Mouse's older brother, regaled her with stories of fighting off tunnel rats like a Ninja Turtle.

"Three or four years now," I told her, "Or maybe less. It's been a long time. What year is it?" I asked her.

"Uh..." she told me and I shook my head.

"Two and a half years. Wow, I thought it was longer."

"How can you not remember something like that?" she asked me.

"I quit caring about life. Got into some bad stuff," I told her.

"Were you hiding from the police?"

"No, I just... quit caring about being alive for a while."

The group of kids and young adults suddenly grew silent and they all looked at me.

"He never talks about the 'before,'" Mouse said, scooting closer to my side until I could feel the burning heat coming off of her body.

"Before I forget, little Door Mouse, I have medicine for you," I said fishing in my pocket, almost spilling the bowl of stew I had in my lap.

We were almost all sitting Indian style, but Jeremy was standing near the small step to the mez where we were all resting. I straightened my leg out enough to get the envelope out, and I fished out a pill.

"Swallow that," I told her, "One in the morning, one at night," then I closed the envelope and tossed it to Danielle.

She would remember for me. Mouse took a slurp of soup and then put the pill in her mouth and made a face as she swallowed it.

"You were going to talk about before," Pauly said, putting his bowl down.

"Well, I wasn't wanting to…"

"Come on," the little kids begged.

"I don't know if that's a good idea," Jamie said.

I didn't blame her. I had basically been admitting I had been having suicidal thoughts.

"Yeah, nobody wants to hear about that," I agreed.

"Oh, I sort of do," Danielle said, standing and walking over to Jeremy, putting an arm around his waist.

His eyes shot open and some of the younger kids laughed and snickered, but nobody said anything about it. It had been obvious that Jeremy had had a 'thing' for Danielle for a long time. Danielle had finally noticed when she realized he wasn't being standoffish to her on purpose, but was trying to mask his feelings. Still, it was the first sort of contact. Both of them were actually eighteen or nineteen, still kids, but old enough.

"Ok, I won't tell the bad stuff, but what do you want to know?" I asked them.

"Why do you have bad dreams at night?" Mouse said, "You pretend to be so mean, but you get bad dreams and cry sometimes when you're sleeping."

"I don't…" but I stopped because all the kids were nodding in agreement with her.

"I don't know if I can talk about that," I said after a few moments.

"You always said that talking about it helps," Jeremy said.

"For conquering your fears, yes," I told him, "If I tell everything, I might just scare the little ones," I said, hoping he'd drop it.

"What if you tell the parts that aren't scary?" Mel asked.

Now what the hell was going on?

"I don't know how to separate out the good and the bad," I said after a minute.

"What did you used to do for a living?" Danielle asked, "You weren't no preacher, that's for sure."

Chuckles broke out around the room. Every single one of them had known violence of some sort. I'd had to deal a ton of it out to secure their freedom. Sometimes, it caused loss of life. Sometimes, I'd had to send a message. Nobody here was truly innocent anymore. Even little Mouse, who was so scared of men that she preferred living underground with our misfit family.

"Well," I said considering my words, "I was an active duty Marine for twenty-two years, a Devil Dog—"

"Like a mean junkyard dog, like you said before?" Sarah asked the nine-year-old who'd joined us a week before.

"No, I was a soldier. Devil Dog's a nickname for a Marine," I told her, "I was in every sandbox and hellhole in the world, but the worst was in Fallujah. After I got a medical discharge, I worked for the

Transit Authority."

"What's that?" Pauly asked.

"Yeah, what's that?" Mouse piped up.

"Well, I was like a railroad cop," I told them, hoping to skip the discharge conversation entirely.

"Oh, did you have to arrest the trains?" she asked me.

I grinned at that, it was too cute. "No, mostly I kept an eye on the tunnels and kept kids from… well, doing what we're doing. Living down here."

"How come?" Seth asked. He was about twelve if I could remember correctly.

"Well, it's dangerous," I said immediately.

"Then why are we down here?" Jamie asked me, arching an eyebrow, a smile tugging the corner of her mouth.

"Because it's more dangerous topside right now, especially for women and children," I said, changing the subject. "You two aren't from around here. Your accent is a little different."

"Change the subject much?" Mel asked, but she wasn't upset, just wise to what I was doing.

"Ok, a little bit, but what about you two? I know almost nothing about you."

"Well," Jamie said, after exchanging glances with her daughter, "We're on our way home."

"Oh, where's that?" I asked them.

"Near Lincoln, Nebraska," Mel answered for her mom.

"Oh wow, you got stuck a long way away, huh?"

"Yeah, we've been traveling for about a month now," Jamie said, "Got stupid, tried to cut through the city here. My husband warned me this would happen someday and to avoid the big cities, but I wouldn't listen to him." Jamie had started crying softly, tears running down one side of her face.

She must have been holding it back for a long while, but her composure had cracked completely and she started sobbing. Mel put her arm around her mom and leaned in with her head resting on her mom's arm. Mouse, on the other hand, coughed hard, then gave her bowl to her brother and got up and walked over, plopping herself down in Jamie's lap. Jamie let out a surprised squeak, and Mouse produced a hairbrush. Like magic, Jamie took the brush and started combing the young girl's hair, and the crying dried up.

"She's a smart kid," Jeremy said.

"Think she rehearsed that?" Danielle asked.

"She does it to Dick all the time," he answered her.

"I never noticed," Danielle told him back, letting him go and walking back to her spot and sat down.

"Yeah," I admitted, "It's her evil superpower. She stops tears and gets her hair brushed at the same time."

"It's a perfect superpower," Mouse said, "Plus it feels good," she leaned back into Jamie's arms, making her stop brushing the back, so she moved to the front and sides.

"So, everyone down here," Mel asked, "Did Dick rescue all of you?"

Everyone fell silent, the usual hum and buzz cut

off.

"One way or another," Jeremy said, "More than half of us were taken from the gangs, a couple of us were sick. Um… I found my way down here after watching Dick come and go, never seeming to get skinnier. I was hungry and…"

"I almost knifed him when I found him following me," I told them, "Then up close, I realized he was just a kid. We talked, and he came down here to help me keep an eye on things. Run the partial trap line like Danielle does," I said, motioning with my spoon to her. "Not everyone stays. Folks leave more than they stay."

"So, why is it that they hate you topside so much? This gang?" Mel asked, and her mother nodded as well, as if to congratulate her on the question.

"I don't know much about the gang. There's always too many to keep one alive long enough to question him. I know the smaller gangs snatch people. Mostly women and kids. We know what happens to at least some of those taken…" My words trailed off, as I imagined what the creep was planning to do to Maggie… Mel. I rubbed my temples. "And whenever I find them, I do what I need to do."

"You kill them?" Jamie asked.

"Yeah, sometimes, when there's no other choice."

"You just mow them down, like Mom said you did to the three guys who took us?" Mel asked, rubbing at her own temples now.

"If there's no sneaky way of getting you free. But I'm not about to let something happen to anybody because it was dangerous to me. These two," I said pointing out Danielle and Jeremy, "run things down here."

"You started this family," Danielle said, smirking.

"It just sort of happened. I helped people. That's what I've got left in me. It's what I can do," I told them.

"What about your daughter, Maggie?" Jamie asked.

I winced. What about her? Did Mary and Maggie make it to her parents' farm? A thousand questions ran through my mind, and I didn't know what the real answer was.

"She should be ok. I'm going to head out some time to find her, but there's so much to do here…" I stopped.

Mouse got up and pulled her brush out, and when she plopped in my lap she almost crushed the delicate parts of me, and I grimaced for a second before taking the brush.

"He's good at it," Mouse told the group of us and the kids laughed knowingly.

I brushed her hair slowly.

"You know," Jeremy said, "Nobody here would blame you for wanting to go find your own family. I think it might help you, you know? Every time we believe that you're about ready to head out, you bring someone else back," he said, and most of the little ones nodded.

"We'd miss you, though. Even if you do talk in your sleep," Danielle said.

"And make stinky farts," Pauly piped up, and we all grinned at that.

"I wasn't the one who ate a whole can of beans and had to sit on the bucket half the day, Mr. Pauly," I told him grinning.

"Beans, beans, the musical fruit..." came from my lap and I smiled again.

I remembered who I was, where I was, and what I was doing. I'd saved two people today, stopping some bad stuff from happening. Mel took our bowls and Jamie handed me a blanket. I looked at her, puzzled. She pointed down. Somewhere in my thoughts, I'd kept brushing Mouse's hair, but the little girl had fallen asleep. I lifted her off my lap carefully and put her on the blanket, tucking her in.

"Is there a bathroom around here?" Melanie asked, looking at me uncomfortably.

"Yeah, come on, I'll show you two where it is. We have to douse most of these lights soon. The kids are going to drift off."

"Ok," Jamie said standing, "Hey, where is your little girl at?"

"Outside Fayetteville, Arkansas," I said.

"That's on the way," Mel said, "To where we're going."

I stopped walking and in the gloom, one of them walked right into my back.

"You really shouldn't leave yet. Give it a week or so," I told her after starting to walk again.

"You really miss Maggie, don't you?" Mel asked.

"I do, I see her everywhere. Every girl her age reminds me of her," I admitted.

"I miss my Dad. I can't wait to finally get home to see him."

"Just give it a week or so, for those topside to let things die down. Even the little market is going to be too hot for me to go to for a while," I told them.

"Market?" They both asked.

"There's a lot to fill you in on," I said, pausing by a curtain which covered up the end of the tunnel.

"There's a toilet seat on a bucket. Liquids in one bucket, solids in another. Cover the solids with some sawdust that's in the last bucket. I can leave the light here, or I can wait. It's up to you two."

"We can manage if you'll leave us a light," Jamie said.

"Yeah, my mom doesn't want you to hear her poop."

"Girls don't poop," both Jamie and I chorused and then laughed.

Mel made a face at me, took the light and stormed into the curtained-off portion. I took that as my cue to leave and I waved to Jamie and strode back to the mez, where I would wait in my hammock for sleep, or nightmares. One or the other.

CHAPTER 4

I woke up in agony. My lower back was killing me. I had to piss something fierce, but I couldn't straighten out enough to swing my legs over the side of the hammock. I groaned loudly, my body breaking out into a sweat as the pain kicked in.

"What's wrong, Uncle Dick?" Mouse asked, walking up timidly.

It didn't matter how early or late she went to bed, she would always be the first one up, and ninety-nine percent of the time, she'd be cheerful. This didn't look like one of those times. Her eyes were dark and hollow looking. I know what that haunted look meant. I'd seen it in the mirror enough times myself. Nightmares, ones that scare you awake, and haunt you until the sunlight burns the horrors away. It sucked because there was no sunlight here.

"Back," I gasped.

"Well, let me get your feet," she said, pulling.

I gasped and I saw Jeremy startle awake. His spot was close to mine, near the entrance to the small chamber. He stood up, stretching. I could hear his joints pop and crackle.

"You ok?" He asked.

"Back hurts," I told him. "Help me up."

He did and it was agonizing, and when I made it to my feet, I was hunched over. It took me almost a minute to stand up straight. Like him, several sections of my back popped, but a hot ball of pain was still centered in the middle of it. I kneaded it and wandered down the tunnel to do my business.

When I got back, almost everyone was getting up or waking up. Those who were up were taking the sleeping pads and sleeping mats we'd fashioned from a school's rubber wrestling mats, and stacking them on one side. The kids, young and old, folded or rolled up their blankets. Everyone knew which ones were theirs.

"What's wrong with you?" Danielle asked, after eyeballing me from across the room and joining me as I stretched by the mez.

"Don't know, pulled something in my back," I told her.

"Want me to get Jeremy to crack it?" she asked me.

"Yeah, that's great," I told her and watched the young lady walk casually across the small room to kneel and talk to him.

She whispered to him and I could see her motion with her head. Still, I kept stretching, knowing he was coming. I'd had it happen before, and it had taken me a couple of days of stretches and exercise to feel like I could breathe without it hurting. But this was worse, much worse.

"Hey, what's wrong?" Jamie said coming over.

Not far behind her, Melanie followed, her hair still smashed on one side of her head from sleep, and a bruise had formed overnight where she'd taken the blow. I probably should have checked her for a concussion, kept waking her up to check on her, but I'd screwed up. I was worried about getting them here and about having another… episode? It had been bad after the divorce, but it had gotten much, much worse after the power went out as a nation. Everywhere I looked, I saw my daughter. Everywhere I went, I was reminded of some place or some time, and I wished I was back with Mary and Maggie, running from my dreams.

"Mouse was right," Mel said, "You cry and talk in your sleep."

That felt like someone had dumped a bucket of ice water over my head.

"What?" I asked her.

"Not that much," Jamie explained, "It's just a new place, it's hard to sleep. Plus, it kind of stinks down here. What's going on with you, you look like you're in pain?"

"Back is acting up," I told her, feeling like the old man I must look like.

"I'm sorry, that's my fault," Mel said, "If you hadn't had to have carried me most of the way…"

"It could have been the fall too," I told her, "Besides, you wouldn't want to be stuck with those guys topside. That's for damn sure."

"Do you have any pain medicine? I've got a few Tylenol 3s with codeine?" Jamie offered, digging in a pocket.

My mouth went dry, and I nodded. I did want those, even if there were only a few. A few would be enough to fix up my back, and help me regain my focus. Maybe I wouldn't have such horrible dreams at night and—

"Don't," Jeremy said, putting his hand over Jamie's, who had found the bottle and was taking the cap off.

"Huh? Why? He's hurt," Mel asked, a confused look on her face.

"He's got… He can't have booze or anything that'll act as a painkiller, except Tylenol, Motrin, Ibuprofen. He's been clean a long time now."

And fate had kept me that way. My God, I almost had caved in again!

"Oh, yeah, I can't have codeine," I told Jamie, who had started putting away the bottle.

"Allergies?" Jamie asked.

"Addiction," I told her, hating the way it sounded.

I won't tell you that I wasn't surprised to see the shocked looks on the newcomers' faces, but there it was. Admit to being a junkie, suddenly your IQ lowers and everything you do is viewed through a lens of suspicion.

"Oh, I'm sorry, I didn't know. How long?" Jamie

asked.

"It's been over a month for him since he's had anything," Danielle said. "He got dinged in the side by one of the topside gangs and his doctor friend had to give him a shot for the pain, so she could dig the bullet out. It couldn't be helped... No booze, no meds like that unless it's life endangering. After that shot of morphine, he almost lost it again."

"Turn around," Jeremy said. "Hold your arms in front of you, hands under chin, elbows together.

I did and I knew it was going to hurt, so while Danielle explained my shortcomings to Jamie and Mel, Jeremy came up behind me, wrapped his arms around me in a bear hug, locking his wrists together and leaned back. His young body supported my weight, but what was interesting was, as my feet left the floor, my own body weight pulled down on my spine, and I felt and heard several pops, one of which was in the area of the worst pain. Immediately, it felt like a dam had burst.

So, it hadn't been a muscle strain, entirely. I was betting the fall had done that to me. The pop must have been loud enough to hear because the three ladies stopped and looked at me in sympathy. Jeremy lowered me to the floor, and I turned to see him grinning.

"How's that?" he asked, getting an appreciative smile from Danielle.

"Good," I told him. "Hurts, but I think you got it. I'm going to lay flat on my back for a minute," I said to him, lying on a dry section of concrete.

Mel knelt down, ignoring Jamie, Danielle, and

Jeremy, who had wandered away to talk.

"Do you really think we should wait a bit before we go back up?" she asked me.

"Yeah," I told her, "Those guys will be hunting all over the city for us. This isn't the first time I've done this to them."

"Why do they do it?" Mel asked suddenly.

"What are we exactly talking about?" I asked her, not comfortable with where I thought the conversation was going.

"Why do they kidnap women and kids?"

In the darkened room, I could make out her features perfectly. She was horror-stricken and afraid. Of whom, I wasn't sure. The situation? The men above, or how easily and quickly society had fallen apart? Her question, though, was hard for me to answer.

"To some people, having control is more of a drug than any booze or meds are. Think about all the power-hungry men in the world that you've heard about in school. They lust to control things they can't have or shouldn't have. Before we grew as a society of laws, the bad people like that were usually put down when they were found… or they recognized that what they wanted wasn't going to fly with the people they were around and they changed. With the collapse of the nation, everyone got a free pass. They went crazy with booze, looting, rioting, drugs and immoral acts."

"I'm guessing you were pretty safe down here when it all went down?" she asked, sitting on the edge of the mez by the concrete I was laying on.

It put her comfortably in my view, so I didn't have to strain to look at her. Thoughtful kid.

"I'll admit, I got all the booze and junk I could, and had my own pity party. An end of the world party to end all parties. I lived through it, though. That wasn't my intention." The words slipped out before I could take them back, but she nodded.

"We ran into many people like that on our way across the country," she said.

The conversation with the others had broken off, and Jeremy was set to go out and check all of the snares. Danielle would be firing up the cook stove and she'd get the never ending soup going again, getting the kids fed before they would break up into groups and practice their reading. All of this had been explained to Jamie as I was talking to Mel, and I'd only paid half attention to their explanations because I'd done it and lived its reality for a long time now.

"How did those guys end up?" I asked her.

"Most of the time, they died on their own terms," Mel told me.

I wasn't the only one who could listen and follow more than one conversation at a time.

"That sucks," I told her, for lack of anything else to say.

That hit Mel as funny, and she snorted.

"What sucks is having what we did for dinner last night," Mel told me.

"I thought it was pretty good, better than those MREs that your dad put in our get-me-home bags," Jamie said, rejoining our conversation.

"Yeah, but that was like… a Rottweiler or something, wasn't it?" Mel asked, "He could have made a good guard dog."

"It was too late for that," I told them. "He got into the snare and was dead in less than a minute. The wire pinched off the blood flow to his brain and he just went to sleep."

"We've done it, Mom and I… the first time was horrible, and the second time was a little bit easier," Mel said.

"Yeah, it's one thing to have a get-me-home bag packed for everything, but not having enough food and water wasn't something we planned on."

"Where were you both at, when the EMP was let off?" I asked them.

"Staying with a friend in Michigan. She'd set up a new farm and we were helping her and her husband move in."

"Why didn't you stay there?" I asked her.

"It's… I don't know if you would believe me. Michigan is bad. It's going to be bad here too, soon." Jamie said, "That's why we were so anxious to move and not wanting to wait things out. It's why we cut through Chicago when we should have spent an extra week avoiding it."

"What do you mean it's bad? I haven't heard anything."

"You remember the riots in LA a bunch of years ago?" she asked me.

I sat up; the cold concrete had worked like a charm on my sore muscles. I was stiff, but the cool had hopefully kept any of the muscles from tightening the wrong way and had given my spine some time to stay straight. Jamie offered me a hand, and I was surprised that the raven-haired woman was as strong as she was. I was pulled upright and I sat down next to them.

"Yeah, I was out of the country when that happened. Saw news footage, though. Was that what happened up north?" I asked her, curious.

"Pretty much," Mel said, "but then there were small groups blowing things up and shooting at people from a long ways off."

"Why, what?" I asked them, confused.

Things had gone to shit, and I'd been in countries where the government had fallen, or their monetary system had collapsed, but to go from looting to total hunting and killing people? For what?

"There were rumors…" Jamie said, "People who had student visas who just never left. Terrorists. When the people in the cities found out, it was horrible. Like… and all-out war zone."

"Terrorists?" I asked them, unbelieving.

"Why not? They kept saying our borders are porous in the southwest. To think we had them in the country all along isn't all that surprising, is it?"

"I guess not," I admitted, "What happened to them? Your friends, I mean. You left. There had to be a reason."

Mel looked at me and shook her head, but it was Jamie who answered me. "There wasn't even that much food on the farm," she said, tears forming in her eyes, "we had gotten away into the woods, hidden out. They… there was nothing left when they moved on… it was a large group of people from the city who were hungry. Our friends didn't have a chance."

"Your friends were killed?" I asked her, and they both nodded. "I'm sorry. What about your husband, why didn't he come on the trip?" I asked.

"He had a work thing. He was going to join us in a week, but… that didn't happen. We waited around a while, hoping he'd come and get us. I knew if things got bad we'd have to move. He had talked about it, he kept telling us something bad would happen someday, and I didn't want to bring the packs," her words sped up as a fat tear slid down her cheek. "And I used to think he was crazy, all this prepping, putting up so much food… getting ready for something that I never thought would happen. I even called him crazy, right before we left, for making us pack those bags. I figured it was too much."

Mel wrapped an arm around her mom and rested her head against her shoulder. Jamie either had to put an arm around her teenaged daughter or risk losing balance, so she did the former. I smiled, noting that it was a move that Mouse would have approved of. As it was, I rose and looked around. I saw Mouse making a face and then sticking her tongue out at Danielle, shaking her head.

"Looks like Mouse doesn't want to take her medicine," I said, stretching again.

"What's her story?" Mel asked, "I mean... her name isn't really Mouse is it?"

"I doubt it. Says she can't remember. Pauly, her brother, won't tell us, or doesn't know himself." I explained.

"How can that be?" Jamie asked me.

"I… Oh, hell, they'll tell you. I got them out of a… house of ill repute. They'd been there a week, been used pretty badly. I wasn't sure Mouse was going to make it. She's had a delicate immune system ever since. This air down here isn't any good for her or any of them."

"Why down here?" Mel asked.

"Well, it's familiar," I told her, "I know these tunnels better than most people nowadays. I can move around the city without having to go topside until the last minute, and when the fires happened, and the planes crashed, I was safe from the fire and toxic fumes."

"Planes crashed?" Mel asked.

"Yeah, I don't know if the EMP knocked out their electronics, or they just tried to land without instruments and a control tower, but we had two or three plane crashes in the city. A couple of gas stations went up like bombs. I guess in some places, the asphalt was burning for days. Pretty horrible stuff."

"So, you didn't really have a choice of going topside?" Jamie asked, wiping her eyes.

"Well, I'd already been down here, living," I admitted, "but topside, things are even more dangerous than they were before. There's three gangs that I know of, operating around the outside edges of downtown. There's somebody near the shipping docks that's buying up all the ladies and kids they can… but I can't get anywhere close to there."

"How come?" Mel asked.

"They're near the docks, not at them, and they always seem to move. Lots of men, lots of guns. More than the idiots who snatched you. These guys know what they are doing."

"So do you," Mel said, letting her mom go and standing up.

"Yeah, but I'm just a broken-down homeless bum," I told her.

"You weren't always. What you did for us yesterday… I don't know how many people would do that."

"That's because you don't know many people," her mom said, nudging her and standing herself.

I smiled, they hadn't been broken, they still had their playful natures. I'd often wondered what would happen to a family that was suddenly thrust together, having to work, live and depend on each other if something happened.

"There's a nice lady topside, a doctor, who has been bugging me for a long time now to get Mouse topside. The poor girl is terrified of going up, so I had the doc come down with me. She… well… the doc is claustrophobic. So we're kind of at a standstill."

"She's your buddy, though, calls you Uncle Dick," Danielle reminded me, walking up, "you want her to leave?"

"I don't want her to go so much as I want her to live," I said softly. "There's something broken inside of Mouse, more than her bad immune system. It's broke up here," I said pointing to my head. "Plus, I know she's never going to get completely better if I keep her down here. I've been trying to convince her to come up with me and meet the doctor again..."

"Maybe we can help with that," Jamie said and turned to walk towards the cooking area, where the smells of warm food had started permeating the air.

Mel gave me a shrug and followed her.

* * *

I knew I should be resting, but I was restless. I had to move. It'd been a long time since I'd had a proper shower or bath, but I was going towards what I considered the next best thing. It was a little bit outside of the tunnel and room we called 'home', but it held something that was priceless. A pipe that ran from the big lake and supplied water to the city had a small leak. Someday, the pipe would rust out, and it would become a big leak or a big flood. I wasn't worried about that so much as getting the stink off of me when it finally happened.

I closed the hatch and turned the lock, so somebody didn't walk in, and

I stripped, putting a bar of soap near the small LED flashlight. It wasn't aimed at the little spray of water, but it was enough light for me to see what I was doing. This time of year, the lake wasn't horribly cold, but cold is a relative term. When the water is sixty degrees in the lower thermal layers where the pipes are, that's what comes out in the spray. I grabbed the bar of soap and stepped in.

I washed up, taking several minutes to check out any bumps, bruises, and scrapes. I could probably get antibiotics all day long, but preventing an infection would be the most important thing I could think of. Still…

Somebody knocked on the hatch behind me.

"Hold on, I'm in here," I shouted back.

We'd left the flood control valve on the other side open, so people could hear beyond the waterproof hatch.

"k……" I heard faintly.

I finished up and dried off. Not having a good laundromat, the sun and wind would dry my clothing, and it made for some interesting ways of keeping clean clothes, but it was a constant battle. If you lived underground, you'd take on the musty, wet smell of damp concrete. A fact of life. When I was done, I undid the hatch and stepped out.

Leaning against the wall was Danielle, her leg behind her, flat against the wall. I could tell by the look she was giving me that she was up to no good.

"So… what's with you and the new girl?" she asked.

That stopped me cold. Mel? Jamie? What?

"What are you talking about?" I asked her.

"Oh, I don't know. I figured that since you seemed to want to point out the obvious to me, I should do some of the same to you," she said, her lips and nose twitching into a smirk.

"Oh, there's nothing between us," I told her. "She's married. Besides, someday Mary and I will…"

"Oh God, don't do this again," she said throwing her hands up in the air in frustration. "We all know that isn't going to happen."

"Just because I still love her, doesn't mean I have to get back together with her. I've had a lot of time to think, to see how much I've screwed up. If I could find her and Maggie, and tell them how sorry I am…"

"You really miss them, don't you?" she asked.

"Yeah," I admitted. "Badly."

"Why don't you go find them? I know you're as good as anybody topside, better probably."

"But I've got responsibilities here. I've got to take care of you guys… and Mouse is sick, and there's those sick fucks that need to be dealt with."

"So deal with them," Danielle said. "Then, go find your family. I swear this is what's driving you crazy, Dick."

"But who'll take care of you guys? I mean, it's not as if—"

"I've been talking to Jeremy about this for a long time now. I don't want to live down here forever, most of us don't. I don't think you do either."

"No….?" I said not knowing where she was going, not sure if I wanted to hear.

"All of us have family somewhere… But look at it this way. What would happen to us if you got hurt and couldn't go topside or go out?"

"Well, you and Jeremy have handled those situations before."

"Yeah, we have. That's the point. If finding Mary and Maggie is going to make you whole again, why not try it? I mean, you can always come back."

It hit me then, why I'd been making excuses. Why I hadn't gone sooner. Yes, what I was doing was necessary and important work, but Danielle was also right. I was doing small hit and grab jobs. If I really wanted to make a difference in the city above, I had to do more than that. I had to bring the war to them - and in a big way. I'd been afraid. My own fear had crippled me. My own fear had kept me from finally wiping out the guys who were preying on others. Who knew what it would be like to do it, and then get on the road to go see Maggie, the *real* Maggie… not every fourteen or fifteen-year-old girl who somewhat resembled her?

"I'll think about it," was what I told her, but she smiled and handed me a dirty plastic bag.

"What is that?" I asked her.

"Open it up. Maybe a new you will make you feel better. You don't have to if you don't want to. Just a thought."

With that, she walked away from me, whistling some video game tune. I opened the bag and let out a surprised bark of a laugh. A can of shaving cream, scissors, a straight razor and a small pedestal make-up mirror, large enough to show the person's whole face. Maybe the kid was right. Maybe there was a lot of bullshit I'd kept feeding myself, making excuses.

I headed back into the room with the water spray and took care of getting rid of the almost three-year-old beard that had started going gray in long streaks.

CHAPTER 5

I walked back towards our camp, the pen light illuminating the path for me. I hadn't had a smooth face in a long time, and even though I'd thought Danielle had wanted to play matchmaker for me, I hadn't shaved off my beard for Jamie or for Danielle. I'd done it because a new me could be anything and anyone. The fact that it took away one of my most memorable features and made me harder to identify was a bonus.

A new face would give me a chance to start over, but did I want to start over? I'd been living this way for so long now. I didn't know if I ever wanted to go back to the way I was. I did know that I had the capability of stopping the game, even if it was only one at a time. I could pick them off little by little. I could end the reign of terror that they held over the city. I had a few somethings they didn't: knowledge, determination, and experience.

All I had to do was swallow my own fears. I had to keep it together long enough to make a difference. I knew the kids down here thought I was something special, but I wasn't half the man they believed me to be. I needed to be the man that I used to be once again. I needed to be the man that was willing to fight and die for his country. But… I also needed to be the father that I'd never been. To fix my life, my mind, my soul, I needed to make things right with everything and everyone.

Jeremy was the first one to see me as I came out of the tunnel and into the soft glow of the lanterns in our main room. He did a double take at first, his face showing signs of alarm and then he smiled at me and relaxed. Danielle was the next one to notice, and she gave me a grin and a quick thumbs up. What I didn't expect was for Mouse to take one look at me, scream, and go running in the other direction.

"Is there…?" asked Jamie. "Don't worry, I'll go get her… You just… Yeah. Never mind. I've got her."

"Mouse!" The word coming out of my mouth was loud, sharp and commanding.

She must've recognized something because she faltered and then looked over her shoulder. The questioning look in her eyes was mixed with the fear she held for all men.

"Don't worry, that's Uncle Dick," said Mel.

"No, no, no, no, no, no, no..." Mouse started to say, and then she paused, and looked back up at me.

"It really is me, little dormouse," I told her, staying rooted to the spot so I wouldn't scare her. "I just had to trim my beard, and I needed to shave it off."

She had still been moving at that point, but Mel caught up with her and held her hand out. Mouse took it reluctantly and slowed to a walk. She turned around and looked at me again. Mel knelt down close to her and whispered into her ear. Mouse's look of fear melted into a grin and when Mel whispered something else, the little girl started to giggle. She shyly started walking in my direction.

"Well, well, well," Danielle said. "Looks like you clean up good, sir."

"Don't call me sir, I used to work for a living," I said to her, grinning.

"Yeah, that is a new look for you," Jeremy said. "Almost like you plan on going incognito topside."

"Yeah, about that… I've been hiding down here for a long time. Instead of trying to catch the guys before it's too late, I think it's time to bring the fight to them," I said, looking around at the group of kids standing before me. Some of them were playing, some of them sitting. Some of them were reading the books they'd brought down in the tunnels with them. "I don't think it's feasible to get rid of all of them, but the ones who are trying to take the women and children… those I can do something about. If we break the backs of the biggest gangs topside, then we can move around in the open more."

"Uncle Dick, is it really you?" Mouse asked as Mel brought her close to me.

I knelt down. "It's really me, little dormouse.

Who did you think I was? The boogeyman?"

"It really is you!" she exclaimed, letting go of Mel's hand, and running and jumping at the last moment, so I was forced to catch her. I did, and I almost crumbled immediately.

The twinge in my back was something horrible, and even catching a small girl put a strain on it. I felt like screaming. Instead, I put down Mouse. I got down on one knee, feeling everything in my body crack and pop. It sounded like a cross between a bone breaking and glass shattering, but it felt good despite the pain.

"Yeah little one, it's really me. What you think of my new look?" I asked her, pulling her tight and giving her a hug.

She was still warm to the touch, and she coughed. When she spoke, her voice came out still sounding phlegmy and nasally.

"You look like someone my mom would date," Mouse said with a grin, and Pauly started laughing from the mezzanine.

"You know, you didn't have to get all spiffed up for me," Jamie said, and then laughed when Mel slugged her mom in the arm.

"I wasn't doing this to impress anyone, but I feel honored you thought it was all in for you," I said with a grin, noticing the look Mel was shooting her mom. I laughed, "No, I'm just kidding."

Jamie said, "But you had at least a few years' worth of beard. There had to be a reason why you cut it off now?"

"Listen, there's something I've been wanting to

talk to everyone about here. Part of the reason we're all still down here and not topside is because of the gangs that are topside. Some of them would snatch the women and children up right away. The other reason we've stayed down here so much is because half the city wants me dead."

"Why would they want you dead?" Mel asked me.

"Because," Danielle said, walking up towards us to get a better look at my mug, "when everyone started going crazy and hurting people, he put a stop to it. The people he killed. They deserved it, but they had friends and a lot of them have long memories."

"Let me get this right, just because you helped other people and stopped them from hurting others, there's a lot of people in this town that don't like you?" Jamie asked.

"Yeah… Pretty much just like that."

Our conversation was cut off. Up to that point, the other kids had been hanging in the background looking, but they all came up now to get a good look at me. Apparently, shaving off the salt-and-pepper colored beard had transformed me into someone they didn't recognize at first. I half expected a fearful reaction like what I'd gotten with Mouse, but they were more amused or showed no fear at all. I smiled when Jeremy walked up and put an arm around Danielle's waist. She shot him a look, but she didn't move his hand.

"So, boss, do you have a plan?" Jeremy asked me.

"Yeah, I do have a plan. I wanted to run it by you guys because if you had the choice, would you rather stay here or would you rather live topside?"

* * *

We sat and talked about it. Even though I'd done a lot of good for a lot of the kids, overwhelmingly, they wanted to live back among other people again. That hurt at first, but I knew it was selfish to keep them down here, just because they were associated with me. If I had to leave the area and leave them, in order for them to have a safe and happy life, I was willing to do that. And in the back of my mind, I knew that if I did leave, I would be free to go find my wife and daughter.

I explained my plan to them and just about every one of the older kids stood up to volunteer their help. There were some things they could do to help, but not much. I might be able to use the help of Danielle, Jeremy, and Jamie, maybe even little Mel, who I'd thought was my Maggie for a time. But nothing dangerous, they wouldn't be on the front lines of anything. They would be… more like support personnel for me. Ready at entrance and extraction points, have supplies staged, overlook tricks and traps and tripwires.

To do all of this, we needed a lot of time to prep for it, and that coincided nicely with me wanting to stay out of sight for at least a week. It would give me a week to work on little Mouse and Pauly and see if they were ready to take that next step of healing.

* * *

As far as plans went, mine was brutally simple. I was going to watch their operations to get an idea of where everyone was set up, and what their strengths were. Then, I'd do what I could to take them out one by one. And I didn't mean just one person at a time. I meant one gang at a time. There was a plague in Chicago, and if I ever wanted to go see my daughter and wife, ex-wife that is, I needed to be able to feel good about handing the torch over to Danielle and Jeremy. They both were already doing the job in all but name. I think the only thing that was holding me back was Mouse and Pauly, who'd really understood a lot of it without the discussion. But having the discussion was something that was long overdue.

Once everything was clear, Jamie, Mel and myself, well…we needed to plan. They wanted to get home to their father and husband. To do that, they needed to go west and a little bit south. For me to find Maggie and Mary, I needed to head west and then a lot further south to Arkansas. They'd be at the farm. They'd be at Mary's parents farm. They had to be. I would've known in my heart if something had happened to either of them.

While my back was sore, the pre-positioning of goods and materials was going to be a little dicey. I actually wouldn't be moving a lot of stuff until I got a pretty good idea about the gang activity topside. I already knew pretty well where one gang was; underneath the theater roughly. The trick was going to be getting in and out.

Jeremy offered to climb up the coal chute and then set up some sort of watch. I nixed that idea right away because he wasn't trained, he wasn't disciplined, and he wasn't ready for that. Besides, I needed supplies. Guns, ammo, and any kind of grenades or explosives. I wasn't going to go after the biggest gang to start, not with only fifty shotgun shells in an old, beat-up tactical shotgun.

It was time to get ready. I just hoped that I was ready enough when the time came.

CHAPTER 6

Mouse's jump into my arms had not, in fact, helped my back as I'd hoped. I spent two days sweating and trying not to ask for the codeine that I knew Jamie had. I took ibuprofen that I'd sent Jeremy topside to barter for with a handwritten note. I'd sent along a small handful of ammunition as payment, and as something to trade for the supplies we were going to be needing. I had a lot of things down here, but there was a ton of things I didn't have.

I had my shotgun, a pistol, and a small stash of supplies that I hadn't ever told anybody about. Other than that, what everyone saw in the chamber with the mezzanine was all of my worldly possessions. The men who had grabbed the ladies was by far the smallest gang, so taking them down was the first thing on my agenda. Having a plan in place to loot their supplies or finding a way to lock them in the vault of the bank for later use was next.

I'd reasoned that they had to have been using the vault as a storage and safe room. It was an ancient bank, a historic landmark, so I was ninety-nine percent sure that the vault had the old cipher style or key style lock. No electronic locking mechanisms. It was brilliant, but if I did things correctly, I would be using their smart idea to further my own goals.

"So, what did you send Jeremy topside to get today?" Danielle asked me, one hand cocked on her hip.

"I need him to scavenge some alcohol or gas, Styrofoam, nails, mouse traps, more wire cable or electrical wire… stuff like that."

"Junk," she said disgustedly. "You sent him topside to get junk? Is it worth the risk?" she asked.

I was a little shocked. She'd always been the short, prickly attitude type of girl, but lately, she'd been warming to me. Somehow, I must have done or said something. Maybe I was leaning on Jeremy for help too much or wasn't appreciative enough… or—

"It's not junk," Pauly said, pulling Mouse with him.

They had just woken up and although the lanterns were on low, I could tell the difference in the way Mouse looked, that the three days' worth of medication had helped tremendously.

"Oh yeah? What is it?" Danielle asked.

"I heard him telling Miss O'Sullivan that he's

making grape napalm," one of the younger boys said proudly.

"Grape?" Mouse asked hopefully.

"Not grape napalm," I told him. "Jellied Napalm," I finished, looking back at Danielle.

Her face had been scrunched up in anger or annoyance, but it smoothed out as she started thinking.

"How does that work?" she asked me.

"Not in front of the little kids," I told her. "Besides, I need to send the little rats into the nearby tunnels to get as many glass bottles as possible today. Not far, just the side tunnel towards the washroom where all the junk washed through the storm drains."

"What about the other stuff?" she asked, "Nails, rat traps, wire?"

"More MacGyver stuff," I told her. "Trust me, if it weren't important for the plan, I wouldn't be sending him up there. Besides, I've been talking with Mouse."

The little girl looked up at me, tears forming in her eyes.

"I'm going to miss you," Mouse said, and Pauly nodded.

"I'm not going to be gone forever and ever," I told her, "I'm just taking care of some bad guys and running them out of town."

"I meant later. When I go and live with Miss Salina."

My heart clenched, and Danielle looked shocked.

"Hey, little one," I said kneeling down. "You know the tunnels down here make you sick. They'll probably make all of us sick someday. I can't live topside and stay in Chicago."

"Cuz of the wicked men…" she said.

Yeah, we'd explained that over and over. As far as she was concerned, she wanted to be wherever Pauly was first, or me second. She'd kind of brightened up when I'd told her that the Doc wanted a daughter and they'd have a mother again. Not much, but she had half smiled like she would be happy, if she'd not been feeling guilty about being happy.

"Yeah, not just them. I have to find Maggie."

Both Danielle and Mouse looked at me and smiled crookedly. Pauly grinned, and two of the older boys, Steve, and Patrick, came up behind him. They were a little older than Pauly, maybe ten years old. Twins. Something that was rare before the power went out, even rarer now.

"The real Maggie this time," Mouse scolded me, then coughed.

"I'm sure that'll help you out a bit," Mel said, walking up as well with her mom following close behind.

"What do you mean?" I asked her, looking at the growing group of humanity now surrounding me.

"With your… I don't know…" she made a circular motion with her finger at her temple.

That might be insulting to some people, but I wasn't insulted. I understood the gesture. It's wasn't that I was actually loony, though. It was that something inside of me was broken and when I was stressed, my wires crossed. That wasn't why I wanted to find my daughter, though, I wanted to find her because I wanted to make things right again. I wanted to do everything I could for her.

"Well, I won't be rescuing ladies and be convinced that they're my Maggie if I have her at my side, now will I?"

"Yeah, my mom was kinda freaked," Mel said, and Jamie let out an exasperated sound.

"Well, you were," she said.

"Ok," I said, redirecting the conversation, "After breakfast, I need you little ones to go on a bottle hunt with Miss Danielle. I need all the glass bottles you can find. We'll need them rinsed out. Can you do that?"

None of them spoke, but Mouse let go of her brother's hand and walked up and hugged my leg, "Ok, Uncle Dick."

The other kids were smiling and nodding.

"If I'm doing the cooking and the scavenger hunt, who's going to do the trap-line?" Danielle asked.

"I'll do it," I told her.

"Can we come along?" Jamie asked, "I don't know these tunnels well enough to go exploring and I don't want to sit here alone when they leave…"

"It's up to you two," I told them. "I'm heading down a different branch, where the storm drains intersect with an old sewer tunnel. Some of it is stinky to get to where we're going."

"It all stinks down here," Mel snarked, and I had to smile at that.

"Besides," I patted her on the shoulder, "My back isn't healed up yet, I need some young arms to do all the hauling for me."

The kid's eyes blazed for a moment and then she just nodded. God, she was fourteen or fifteen going on twenty. It just amazed me that they'd crossed such a distance alone and on foot. Jamie's husband might have been a crazy prepper like she'd insisted, but he'd obviously trained them well. The thing is when it comes to survival, it is more of the mental game than the physical. Sure, physical training is tough to beat, but if the will to live isn't ingrained in your gray matter, it doesn't matter how strong you are, or how much endurance or skilled at hand to hand you are… If you aren't ready or willing to do what it takes, you don't make it.

"Ok," she said, "but you handle any of the gross stuff. I'm still a girl, you know."

"I know it all too well," Jamie said. "Go get your pack, in case we need any of it while we're with Dick."

The small gathering broke up, with the younger kids heading up to the cooking platform on the mez. Danielle, Jeremy, and I all had our own trap lines that provided meat for the group. Jeremy would take care of his on the way back in, while I had promised to do mine and Danielle's.

"So," Jamie said, "I guess this is nothing like hunting and trapping that normal people do."

"No, it isn't," I told her. "I was surprised to find you weren't grossed out that first night here."

I had expected them to vomit or run away from

us, but apparently eating a snared dog hadn't been horrible to them.

"Oh no," Jamie said, "Protein's protein. Once you get past that mental block, it isn't that bad. What did it for you?"

I thought about it a second, "The world turned into a three day, just in time, supply and demand type of thing. It was all scheduled and computerized. I told you about the jets crashing topside, yeah?"

"Yeah, we saw there had been some big fires coming in towards town, but we hadn't been sure what'd caused them until you told us about the crashes."

"Well, the first big die-off topside was from the fires. Then, over the course of two months, deaths were mostly due to starvation, with human predation coming in at a third. All of the food in the city was seemingly consumed within a week. With no more trucks running, food and ammunition became the hottest commodity next to medicines. It was hard to believe how many dogs and cats were just turned loose when their owners couldn't feed them anymore. We were… hungry. I've traveled all over the world and some countries don't have the same taboos about food like Americans do."

"Yeah. My trigger was pretty close to the same. Mel and I hadn't eaten in a few days. We were on the road, just getting near the border in Michigan when we came to a small town. It was dead like, literally. Whoever was left was laying in the middle of the road, and a group of dogs were surrounding the corpse. We couldn't tell what they were doing at first, and when we got close enough to see, we were too close to run far."

"Did you get hurt?" I asked as Mel came back with her pack.

"No, I had Mom climb on top of a semi's hood with me, then we sat up on the box for a long time. Those stupid dogs kept circling it and growling, from the time they'd quit eating to when the sun went down. They all went somewhere, and we got out of there."

"So them eating people, put you onto eating dog?" I asked her, unbelievingly.

"No," Jamie answered. "It showed us that even household pets can turn into predators and that we shouldn't trust them like we would have in earlier times. It was the day after, in another town when we ran across another small pack of them. They'd chased down a deer."

"Mom dropped a rock on the head of one of them," Mel said. "We were so hungry..." She looked at me with a guilty expression.

"Hey kid, I know hunger," I said pointing to my stomach. "Everything looks good when it's sprinkled with starvation. People in our old lives didn't even have a clue what real starvation was like. Now..."

"Everything's different," Jamie finished. "That's why we want to see your trap line. I need to make it home to my husband and if I can help and pick up on some skills while you're healing up..."

"No, it's fine. I just wish I wasn't such a dick-head that they're going to be hunting and gunning for me."

"That's your name, isn't it? Dickhead?" Mel snickered.

"Richard actually, but you can call me Dick, if'n you please," I said with a mock bow.

The move set off a twinge in my back and when I straightened up, I winced in pain.

"Sorry," Mel said.

"It's not your fault," I told her. "I'm just getting old."

* * *

"The trick with rats and dogs is to get the snare set up in the right spot. Dogs down here usually have their noses to the ground, smelling out something to eat. So you put the big part of the loop about three to six inches from the floor." I showed them.

I'd constructed the simple snares from stripped copper cable and an old penny.

"What's that for?" Mel asked, pointing to the penny.

"That's what keeps the animal from backing out," I told her.

"How does that work?" Jamie asked as we were standing in front of the first trap.

I showed them. I'd taken a penny and put it in a vice, hammered one end over at a ninety-degree angle, then put the half bent penny on a piece of wood. I'd punched a small hole on one side with a punch I'd traded for at the market. I made it just large enough so that the stripped wire could move through it. Then, I'd made one on the other side, across from the first hole. I ran the end of a piece of wire into it and then twisted and tied it closed. It made a loop, and when I pulled it tight around Jamie's arm, it didn't let go.

"Huh, that's pretty cool, I guess," Mel told me. "But why don't they just back it off like this?" she asked, taking the penny in her hand and sliding it back, freeing her mother's arm.

"The same reason that humans are top of the food chain, kid."

"Oh yeah? What's that mean?" she asked.

"Opposable thumbs," I said grinning.

"So, do you ever bait these?" Jamie asked me.

"Sometimes, it's just that lately, things have been pretty tight. Not as many animals coming and going."

"You're over-hunting the area," Mel told me. "Like what the DNR said in Michigan when we were asking Lisa's family about hunting."

"Yeah, probably just like that," Jamie agreed, and then to me, "What would you use as bait?"

"Well…" I struggled for the word, to see how squeamish she was. "Rat innards sometimes. Leftover scraps of hide and fur from previous kills. Anything with the scent of blood."

"You know, I hope you get to meet my husband someday. He'd love you," Jamie said, giving my arm a friendly squeeze. "Where's the next one?"

***

"Ok, so why are you pouring that ammonia out?" Jamie said, plugging her nose.

"Just watch, and keep the net ready," I told them.

Angry squeaks echoed and several forms dashed out of the rat hole in the soft sand where the tunnel wall intersected with an old sub-basement of a building. The tunnels were lousy with rat holes the closer to the surface you got, and we were only about ten feet down, in an old forgotten part near the river. The wooden pilings supporting the streets above would have given city engineers heart attacks if they'd realized how much of the structures above were being supported by hundred-year-old timber.

"I hear them, but I don't…"

Several dark forms burst from the rat hole, and both girls dove on the handle of the landing net I'd had them place over the rat hole. Two or three large rats were stuck immediately and before they could turn directions, I gave the signal. They turned the handle and lifted it, swinging the rats away from a quick escape.

"Give them here," I said, picking up a piece of re-bar I'd brought for just this occasion.

Mel was the only one horrified when I hit them once sharply on the head, breaking their necks. I'd had to do it as a matter of protecting my food source before the EMP. Now, they were the food source of sorts.

"Ugggg," Jamie said. "Dog is one thing, but eating rat is another."

"I know," I told her. "The rest of the traps were empty, though."

They had been empty. It had been another busy day. That's why I'd gone to this section of tunnels. It had been lousy with rats and when I'd first moved underground, I'd been driven out by their relentless numbers and the fact they wouldn't leave my food alone. I'd had to go so far as cooking and eating somewhere else until an old hobo had told me about a hundred-ten proof ammonia to run them off. It worked, but it stank. In the end, it was easier just to go somewhere else than always fight them. Now, I was using a slight variation from what the old coot had told me.

"What do you do if the hole doesn't go straight down?" Mel asked, after making a noise that sounded a lot like "gurk."

"I use this," I said, pulling out an old plumber's snake.

"I don't get it?"

Despite her horror, her stomach rumbled, and both me and her mother gave her an amused grin.

"That's ok. This is the easy one."

I unrolled the old school plumbers snake. It was a long flexible piece of metal with a curved hook on the very end. It was easily ten to twelve feet long.

"So, you put that in the hole and go fishing for them? Doesn't that hurt them?" she asked me.

I had thought about it, but I hadn't felt comfortable with it either. I held up the end to show her.

"Soak a rag in ammonia, stick it on the end here, and fish that down the hole. You'll know if there's a critter in there by the sound they make. Just fish the snake in while standing on the landing net. When they come bolting out like these three did, you bop them and Bon appetite."

Again, she made a gagging sound and it almost looked as if she had dry heaves until she slowly straightened up.

"This is so gross," Mel said.

"Keeps us fed," I told her.

"I bet the ladies love you. Fine wine, some cheese, and broiled rat done medium rare," Jamie told me, grinning.

"You're so…" Mel ran to the side of the tunnel and started dry heaving again.

"If you finally get sick, we'll set a trap by it," I told her.

"Just… Stop…" she begged between some wet-sounding burps.

"I'm sorry," I said to Jamie, half laughing. "I haven't… I mean… I know this is bad, but I'm seeing how gross this is through her eyes and it's…"

"None of us would be doing this if the lights were on and Speedway had Tornados, two for $2."

"Exactly," I told her.

"Oh God, don't talk about food," Mel begged.

"You want to try the snake out?" I asked Jamie.

She nodded, and after a bit, her daughter joined her. In a couple of days, we'd be scouting soon, and I'd need everyone's help to do it.

CHAPTER 7

Jeremy made it, but I was almost dancing with worry. I could see Danielle shooting me death glares, but just as I was loading my shotgun, one of the girls came running down the tunnel to announce his arrival, shouting that we'd have a big meal tonight. That brought smiles to everybody's faces. Sure, we'd brought in meat, but nothing excited the kids like a big meal. I held back the urge to go look and see what he'd caught, but when he stepped through the doorway my eyes widened in shock.

A small deer was over his shoulder and he was sweating with the weight of it. Where or how he'd found one, let alone killed it without a gun, boggled the mind. No matter what though, it was a meat that I craved and I could do a lot with it.

"Is that… Oh, wow," Danielle said as he dropped the deer on the concrete near the mez.

"How did you get that?" I asked him, unable to hold back any longer. "And where's the stuff? No luck trading?"

"Oh yeah, I got it all. I just couldn't carry everything at once, so I had to cache some and bring this. I figured the sooner Danielle got cooking…"

She slugged him on the shoulder, but she was smiling at him, "Where did you get it?" she asked.

"I was going through an old house at the edge of town. I was looking for the usual; medicines we could use, more shells… and I saw something flash by me. I figured the house had already been pretty much tossed, cuz I found the door open… so I didn't know if I should bolt out of there or hide, until this one darted past me. It had gotten into the house, so I just closed the door and… I mean, it's here."

I looked at it and didn't see any obvious punctures or shots, so he had to have clubbed it or something else. I looked around, and the kids were staring at it hungrily, so I understood why he didn't just come right out and say it.

"You did good," I told him. "What about the other stuff on the wish list?"

"The bathroom supplies? Yeah, those I got, but I don't know why you want them."

"That's ok," I told him. "As long as you got them."

"Ok, cool. I got them. Hey, I gave the Doc your note. She told me she's ready whenever you are and said she can come down and visit if it would help."

I nodded. I knew it had to be done, and if she were willing to swallow her fears and come down here, I could do the same. I had to do it for Mouse's sake.

"What was in the note?" Danielle asked.

"I told her I talked to Mouse about it, and that she'd like to meet the Doc someday."

"That's what the little squirt was talking about?" Danielle asked, ruffling the kid's tousled hair.

"Don't make me get the brush out!" Mouse told her sternly and I bust up laughing.

I knew the diminutive six-year-old wasn't talking about spanking the almost nineteen-year-old Danielle with it, rather she was mad about her hair… but once the mental image was locked into place, I couldn't hold back. Everyone else except Danielle, was in the same boat, Jeremy included.

"That isn't that funny," Danielle told him.

"It kind of is," he said, rolling his shoulders to loosen the tension.

"Whatever we don't eat tonight, we'll have to get it prepared to save," I told everyone.

"That sounds awesome," Mel said, "What are you going to do? Can it, smoke it, salt it? My dad likes to do a lot of that stuff and he makes some really good jerky…" her words petered out and tears filled her eyes.

We all fell silent at that.

"I'll get going on the deer if you guys want to get the cook fire and the smoker fired up down the tunnel," I told them.

"You have a smoker down here?" Mel asked,

trying to change the subject.

"Yeah," I said smiling, "It's pretty crude, but it works. Want to see it after I butcher the deer and the…?" I motioned to the vermin we had trapped.

"Yeah, I just don't know if I can watch… you know..." she said.

"Did she puke?" Danielle asked wickedly. "When you bopped them?"

"Almost, but it was when her mom started talking about wine, cheese and braised…"

The kid turned green and ran towards the back of the mez with her hands over her ears.

"She's new at this," Jamie admonished me. "She can survive, but that doesn't mean she doesn't get grossed out."

"Yeah, it's a girl thing," Danielle said after a second. "I'll go talk to her."

"Thanks," her mom said and watched as she left. "So Dick, you want a hand with this?"

* * *

"This is the smoker?" Mel asked in disbelief.

"Yup. Beauty, isn't she?"

"It's just a room with coat hangers." The disappointment in her voice was apparent.

"It's not that bad. See? There, we use the coals and wet wood to make the smoke."

"I see that, but… It's not a little box. How is this even… I mean, doesn't it need to be warm to cook the meat?"

"No, with a room this size, it's more like cold

smoking," I told her.

The room was about six feet in diameter and eight feet long. It had watertight access doors on either end. I thought it had been a double failsafe measure put in, so if major flooding happened, it would stop the water before it hit the critical utilities in the section we were in. It was in an older part of the tunnel system, where the construction crews would drill a hole from the street down to make sure the tunnels went in a straight line. This was such a section.

"Look, see that?" I told her pointing out the three-inch diameter hole in the ceiling.

"Yeah?"

"That's one of the holes that was drilled to keep the tunnels straight when they were digging out down here. They left some of them open, so they could get fresh air down here and the air didn't get so bad."

"So that one opens up somewhere?" she asked, looking up.

"Yeah, I think into a sub-basement. There'd be no way for anybody to find us, though. So, it's perfect."

"So… how does the air get in?" Jamie asked, looking in.

"Remember those flood valves under the door hatch?" I asked, thinking I had shown her them.

"Sure, they're kept closed and the door shut. You're supposed to open the small valves to see if the room is flooded, right?" she asked me.

"Yeah. So, what we're going to do, since they are

close to the ground, is open up one side of them up, so the air can flow in. Since it's low to the ground, the smoke doesn't escape all that well."

"Is that a smudge pot?" Jamie asked, pointing to the metal container full of ash.

"I'm not really sure. We've used it, though. It must have been a part of something down here. It's too big and heavy to do more than nudge it around. We let the coals build up and then start adding wood that's been soaked in clean water for our smoke. As long as we don't add too much at once, we can keep it going for a long time."

"And this is where you make your BBQ rat? Who knew that there'd be a gourmet BBQ man living under Chicago," Mel told me, smirking.

"I don't know about all of that, Maggie," I told her "But we load the meat up on the hangers, hang them off the old conduit and get the fire going..."

They were looking at me funny and I had to stop myself.

"I'm sorry," I told them. "I did it again, didn't I, I slipped up. I know you're not Maggie, it's just that..."

God, I felt so stupid. It was bad enough to feel like I'd got a screw loose, but when I acted like it over and over, I started to wonder that maybe I really did have a screw loose. Plus, they both were looking at me in a pitying way. I didn't want their pity. I didn't mean—

"Hey, it's ok," Mel said walking over to me. "If you slip up and call me Maggie, that's cool. You saved us from those guys. I just look at it like, I remind you of your daughter. It doesn't creep me out or anything."

I felt about three-feet tall.

"I know you aren't really Maggie. It was just a slip of the tongue. It wasn't before when I 'knew' you were my daughter, but I was wrong. I was just…"

"Is it PTSD?" Jamie asked me suddenly.

I nodded. It was that and a whole ball of guilt and bottled emotions battling around inside of me, all at once. I felt like I had exposed wiring some days and when I got stressed out... some of the bare wires shorted out on each other. I was never violent, more… confused.

"Didn't the VA try to help you?" Mel's mother asked me again.

"Well, yeah, but getting appointments sucked. I couldn't get in often enough to get my medicine refilled before I'd run out of it. I was already in the process of a divorce and after a while, I stopped caring, I guess," I admitted. "I was too stuck inside of my own head."

"Well, at least some good came out of it," Mel told me brightly and took one of the big platters of meat we'd brought with us.

I stared at her for a second, trying to figure out if she was making fun of me or not. She took down a hanger and started laying the thinly cut strips of meat across them. When she'd finished, she replaced the hanger and got another one. I just stared.

"What?" she asked.

"What good came out of it?" I asked her.

"Well, for whatever reason, God led us to you,

for better or worse. When we needed help, you saved us. By the look of it, you saved a lot of others, too. There were people on the street when we were taken. They scattered and ran away. My mom says when she first saw you, you were running right at the fight and didn't let up until we were safe. So, that might be a little selfish of me, but thank you for being you, no matter what."

In one simple breath of air and a handful of words, the girl had totally disarmed me. I looked her over, cocking my head and considering her words. She was only fourteen or fifteen, but she was way too wise for most kids her age. Hell, that was something I'd never heard from most grown men. One of the psychologists at the VA had gotten through to me and had totally disarmed me the way this young girl had just done, but he'd gotten transferred to Germany and I'd had to start over with a new guy.

"I don't know if I should say thank you or just…" I pulled her close and crushed her with a one-armed hug. "And I'll try not to slip up. I know you aren't my Maggie, just like I know the others aren't. It's just that when I get stressed, I sometimes get my wires crossed."

"I can understand some of that," Jamie said, grabbing a wire hanger and starting to fill it the same as her daughter. "But I can't say that I can understand all of it. It sounds like you've been through a lot in your life."

"Yeah, real life is stranger than fiction sometimes," I told them and started hanging pieces of meat myself.

As a habit, a stack of firewood had been laid out for the next batch of meat. It was pallet wood. I'd found a few junk pallets made out of rough-hewn hickory. When all the meat was hung, I started the fire using a small pile of shavings I'd cut off of a plank. Soon, I was feeding the flames with larger slivers and then as that got going, the planks. The ladies watched with the door mostly closed. In twenty minutes, I had a pretty good fire going. I pulled a piece of scrap metal over three-fourths of the fire and let it go.

"Now what?" Mel asked.

"Now, we have to go get the wood that is soaking and add it to the fire when it dies down a little bit. We'll close off the doors, though. There's some smoke now, but it's going to be more than triple soon."

"Ok, that sounds good to me!" Mel said with a bounce.

I marveled at the kid's resiliency. An hour or two ago, she had been gagging at the thought of the survival meat we'd been fixing to cook up, and now she was hanging it and was ready for whatever else came her way. Jamie must have inferred my thoughts and nodded.

"She's a good kid, strong. She misses her dad, though."

"I'm not holding you two here," I told her, as we started walking.

"Oh, I know, but I agree. If you've caused as much hell 'topside', as you call it, as you're saying you have, it would make sense that they are going to be stirred up. I'm just surprised that you let Jeremy go up so soon."

"They don't know he's with me," I told her. "Just Salina and her son, Jerome, know that."

"Oh, so he's like, your secret spy for topside," she said, grinning.

"Yeah, sometimes. He'll go up sometimes and see who's trying to recruit. Gives us an idea of who to look at."

"You know where all of the gangs are?" she asked, surprised.

"Oh hell, no," I said. "But I know where most of the ones that are into human trafficking are.

I saw her shudder and I looked to see gooseflesh covering her arms.

"You ok?" I asked her, watching her rub her hands over her arms, smoothing the skin back down.

"Yeah, goose walked over my grave. Since when did people turn into such utterly horribly, ugly creatures?"

I paused to see if Mel was far enough ahead and I slowed my pace slightly. Jamie followed suit.

"I think, deep down, more than half of the people out there never think about anybody else other than themselves. When you take away rules and consequences, those half have the great capacity to be evil fucks. It isn't just guys either though it seems like most of the truly evil ones are men by the majority. I've run across some bad women, too."

"Like your ex-wife?" Jamie asked, probably trying to lighten the mood.

"Mary wasn't… I mean… we fought. Mostly about how I'd sign up for another tour somewhere, but that's because I was avoiding her."

"Why?" she asked and then her hand came up to cover her mouth. "I'm sorry, that's too personal. I just… Don't think I'm asking because you're here and my husband isn't…"

"Oh no!" I said starting to laugh. "I didn't think that."

"Oh? You didn't take it well when I teased you the other day."

"I think it surprised me, actually. I'm always surrounded by people a third to only half my age," I said.

She let out a soft laugh herself, "That's why I'm trying to get to know you," she said. "I've lacked adult conversation lately."

"Hey, I welcome the friendship," I told her, watching Mel stop and turn around to see what was taking us so long. "We're the only grownups on the bus. You know?"

"I do," she said. "So, you think that, of the people who've survived, most of them are shitheads, evil, or too scared to act?"

"Yeah, pretty much," I told her.

"Wow, that's… cynical."

"Yeah, I know. Unfortunately, I think it's rubbed off on Danielle."

"What's her story?" she asked me.

"You'll have to ask her. That's not mine to tell."

"Fair enough. Are her and Jeremy… I mean, is

the doctor supplying birth control or…?"

"As far as I know," I said, grossed out, "they've just started showing affection for each other. I think Danielle spent half the time she's been down here, trying to hate him. I think it was the day we brought you two back that she actually started being nice to him."

"It's a girl's tactic. If he can take her at her worst and keep coming back, he's a keeper," she said, grinning.

"Well, shit," I said, slowing down more.

She stopped and turned to face me.

"What?" She asked.

"That's where I screwed up with Mary. I ran."

"How so?" she asked.

"Hey, guys, you coming?" Mel called to us, her voice echoing on the tunnel walls.

"I kept leaving. I could have taken a promotion, got a desk job stateside. I just… I couldn't do it."

"Because you aren't a desk job sort of guy?" she asked me.

"Yeah, war was all I knew. It is… was… what I knew how to do. A wife and daughter? I didn't know what I was doing there. Every time I'd come back, they were a little older and I was more of a stranger to them. It was easier to stay gone," I admitted.

What the hell was happening to me? In the last hour, I'd just figured out the truth. Maybe all it took was a kind ear and time.

"Well, we can always hope that we're not too late to fix things then, right?"

"Lady," I told her starting to walk again. "I can't wait to meet your husband and tell him what a good choice he made in his woman."

"Who said he chose me?" she said and then laughed when my mouth dropped open.

Well, shit, that didn't leave me any words left to use, so I shut my mouth and raised my lantern up a bit and started walking again. I'd have one of the kids run back and keep the fire tended off and on for a couple of days, but other than that… I had some recon to do.

CHAPTER 8

"What you see?" Danielle asked me.

"I see six inside and.... at least three that have left sight. How long have you had eyes on this group?" I asked Danielle.

Yeah, I know. I said I wasn't going to use them but we found a spot where we could come out of the tunnel and escape quickly. It didn't look directly at the old bank building, but it was close enough and a little further down the street than the theater was. It was an area of the underground I was familiar with, and it was one that Danielle and Jeremy had started exploring as well. We were holed up in an old apartment building.

One of the first things we'd done was to go door to door with my lock-pick gun and make sure that very apartment was unoccupied. The fact that half of the building had been cleaved open from a plane's impact would have scared off some, but a safe place was a safe place. The reason I wanted to make sure that the building was empty was simply because I was planning to drop it and burn it down. If it had been occupied, I would have found something very similar to it somewhere else.

The thing that the building had going for it, its greatest asset, was its almost unobstructed view of the street heading towards the old bank where the gang was holed up. It would take a few days to get things set up and we had already started, but if things went down the way I hoped they would, this neck of the neighborhood would be safe at least. We just wanted to make sure that we knew exactly how many there were, and who they were, so we could make sure that we got almost all of them – if not all of them – at once.

Obviously, if they'd snatched someone else, I would've moved a lot faster, but I thought the biggest thing going for me was that they liked to drink. They liked to cause trouble and if they could pick up some extra collateral, they would do so. They were opportunistic predators, and just because they didn't make their entire living kidnapping and subjugating others for their dark carnal lusts, it didn't mean they were innocent. I'd seen with my own eyes what they'd done and what they were willing to do. In my eyes, that made them the perfect target to start with.

* * *

After two more days of careful observation, I'd had everything nailed down. There were nine men left in the gang. We (Danielle, Jeremy and I) saw no evidence of any kidnapped victims. It probably would've been classy to give them target designations, but I wasn't into classy, I just wanted them dead. One thing that was confusing, though, was that during close to four to five days of observation, we hadn't seen any food being brought in or out of there. Since neither of the O'Sullivan women, Jamie and Mel, had been inside of there, we'd been unable to get any sort of idea about the interior layout.

The hardest part of the op was the fact that everyone wanted to help. Everyone over the age of fifteen, and I'd really fought against letting any of them help. But the truth of the matter was, I could do the main part, but I couldn't pull everything off by myself. Yeah, I could've been the one to set the entire trap, but it would've taken a lot longer and there would have been more risk of exposure… But to use the girls as bait? I didn't know if I liked that part of the plan. Danielle insisted that she was the fastest runner out of all of us. If she got them running close enough and they caught sight of me…

"Are you sure I can't talk you out of this?" I asked Danielle.

"Yeah, I'm sure. I know what these guys have probably done, and I know that they're going to keep doing it unless someone stops them. I'm glad you're not too stupid to tell me that I can't help," Danielle told me, with a defiant look in her eye.

"Yeah, as long as you get back to the tunnel

safely, and make sure that Jamie and Mel are ready to go."

"Oh, don't worry about me. As soon as I can get them chasing me, I'll be off like the wind. Once I hear the gunfire and the fireworks, we'll all be ready at different exit points, just in case," Danielle said with a grin.

Danielle had done more than her usual scrub and wash. She'd been holding back some beauty supplies for a special occasion and for once, she was using them to their full effect. Gone was the grubby teenaged girl, the eighteen-year-old teenage girl, and what stood before me was a beautiful young woman. She'd taken the chance to wash and condition her hair, her makeup was applied to effect and from somewhere, someone had found her fresh clothes that had hardly ever been used or worn. What topped off the ensemble, and what made me the most worried, was the four-inch heels she was wearing. I'd never imagined her for the girly girl type. Instead, I always imagined she would be the type to dress in all black and sport Chuck Taylors, but it seemed I was wrong.

Instead, she'd transformed herself into the perfect bait for this crew, and have I mentioned that I hated this part of the plan?

"There's no way you're gonna be able to run in those shoes. Just change out of them, that part's ridiculous," I told her, exasperated, trying to find anything to keep her from getting involved or getting hurt.

I shouldn't have even tried. My efforts were

about as useful as trying to herd cats.

"As soon as they start chasing me, I'm gonna kick them off and I'm gonna run like hell," Danielle told me, with a pouty look.

"There's debris and glass and sharp chunks of concrete everywhere. You could get yourself torn up."

Danielle looked at me for a second and smirked, "You know… I know you think you're all broken and fucked up, but I think you're going to be a really great dad. I think your daughter Maggie is going to appreciate it someday soon."

Part of me smiled, the other part of me kind of felt that one low in the gut, kind of like getting kicked in the nut sack. It hurt, but not in the purely physical I-want-to-puke way. It hurt because maybe she was right, maybe I would've been a great dad. I wanted the chance to find out, and if it meant going through with the plan, which would not only help everyone in the area, but it would also help out with one less group targeting women and children, I would be all for it.

"You're just stalling for time," Danielle told me.

I considered that, and then said, "You know? You might be right, but I don't want anything to happen to you."

"Then, before you say something stupid and get all choked up, let me go do my job. I'll be waiting for you down below when you're done playing around with these assholes," Danielle said with a smirk.

"All right, give me two minutes to get into position and then you go do your thing… don't even enter this building here."

"You just do your thing and you come back to us alive, you got me?" Danielle said and then made a shooing gesture with her hands.

What could I say to that? I gave her a nod and I started walking. I used the shadows made from the afternoon's remaining light until I was in a darkened doorway, just around the corner from the bank. My Keltec KSG had a mixture of rounds in it. The first three rounds were slugs for more long-distance shots. After that, it was an alternating mixture of buckshot and slugs. What made the shotgun different was its capacity and how it held the shells. It was a pump action shotgun that held one in the chamber and six more on each side of the barrel. It was a funny looking space-age type of shotgun, but before the world had gone to shit, and when I was feeling low and trying to cheer myself up, I'd bought one to play with.

On more than one occasion, people would simply think I'd run out of ammunition and pop their head up, only to be plugged, because what shotgun holds more than six or eight rounds? Even the tactical Remington 870 shotguns that the police department used to use didn't hold as many as my Keltec did. The gun had probably been illegal in California and many liberal states, but after the lights went out and the world turned dark around me, who was there to give a shit?

Now that I was in position, all I had to do was wait. On cue, Danielle came walking by, without even looking in my direction. I'd coached her to be very careful not to look at me, or even acknowledge my presence. There was no way I wanted to tip the men off because my hope was that the entire crew wouldn't come right after her at once. I only wanted a few of them to come after her. At the very most. Once my part of the plan kicked off, everyone would come out to play.

"Hey boys," Danielle called. "Do y'all got any food to share?"

"… Don't you come here? … You doing by yourself…" Some voices called out from the distance.

"Just trying to meet all the new neighbors and seeing what a girl's got to do to get a little food in me."

I tensed, as I could see the fake smile on her face start to falter and she lifted one leg pulling off the strap of the heeled shoe and then stepped down. She repeated the process on the other side. You'd have to be as close as I was to see it, but her entire body tensed. I could hear shouts… I'm sure there were words, but I couldn't make them out over the noise of pounding feet. With both shoes in her right hand, Danielle held up three fingers on her left, turned and sprinted. I could hear screams of frustration and anger and I waited, peeking around the corner.

Danielle waited until she'd crossed two buildings in front of me and then darted down an alleyway in front of the trap building. I stepped out of the doorway of the building I'd been hiding in and looked around the corner. To say these guys looked even more homeless than me would've been kind.

Their clothing was a mismatched garble of put-together outfits and clothing that had half rotted or fallen apart.

Their hair was long and unwashed, some of it matted. One thing I didn't see was any emaciated bellies. If anything, these guys looked well fed and healthy, judging by how quickly they were covering the ground. They were in pretty decent shape, all things considered. The apocalypse diet was something I'd learned about a long time before the EMP had taken out the power grid.

Danielle had a pretty good head start on them, and they'd probably expected her to keep running straight down the road, but she was already out of sight and probably less than thirty seconds away from hitting the first entrance to the underground tunnels. I stepped out into the open with a shotgun raised.

I could hear my DI's voice echoing in my head, "*This is my rifle. There are many like it, but this one is mine. My rifle is my best friend. It is my life. I must master it as I must master my life.*"

Two of them kept running while pulling at their sides for the handguns they had holstered there. The third one stuttered to a stop and he started pulling for a long gun that he'd had strapped over his shoulder. Two running men with handguns… fifty yards away… A stationary man with a rifle, he was my first and most dangerous opponent. The boom of shotgun surprised me almost as much is it surprised them, and the man who was holding the rifle flew backward when the heavy twelve-gauge slug tore into his left midsection. I quickly chambered a new shell and fired it. The two men started chasing me.

It should've been an easy shot. It should've been something that I could've done in my sleep. But the adrenaline was kicking in, my heart was racing and my body was acting faster than my brain could react to. It's a weird sort of tunnel vision and I fought against it, so I wouldn't lose perspective. I racked another shell and fired, and one of the men who'd been pulling out a revolver went down in a spray of blood as the flesh of his leg disintegrated from the heavy impact.

"*Without me, my rifle is useless. Without my rifle, I am useless. I must fire my rifle true. I must shoot straighter than my enemy who is trying to kill me. I must shoot him before he shoots me. I will.*" Echoed in my memory.

I started to turn to run just as the last man recognized me, despite my new look. It must have been the shotgun, which was pretty distinctive.

"It's the devil dog!" he screamed as he pulled a 1911 and started firing at me.

There'd been shouts before, but they'd been further off. When I'd started firing, I had tuned all of that out and had focused on the three men, but by the returning shouts and yells, I realized that the rest of the crew had heard him and they were following hot on his heels. I didn't have time, and I knew I would be taking a risk by showing him my back, but I turned and fled. Sparks and chips flew from the asphalt as bullets impacted around my feet and off the stone buildings as I ran past.

My back itched in anticipation of a bullet that never found me. I ran through the front door of the old apartment building and slammed it shut. I kicked a small wedge into the stopped door and then kicked another wooden pole that had been set on the floor. It was holding another wedge in place but from underneath of the floor. The only thing holding up a four-by-four section of the floor underneath the tattered remains of carpet were now three small shims. I'd been careful to run around that. I hazarded a glance out of the side window to make sure that it was all of the men in the gang who were hot on my heels.

"*My rifle and I know that what counts in war is not the rounds we fire, the noise of our burst, nor the smoke we make. We know that it is the hits that count. We will hit.*"

Instead of staying on the first floor, I took to the stairs. I skipped the third, fourth and fifth stair, leaping well over them. It wasn't a lethal trap, but it was something I'd hoped would slow them down. I must admit, watching the movie *Home Alone* was a pretty big inspiration here. Hopefully, these guys weren't any better than the *Wet Bandits* in the movie. By my mental count, I'd downed two of them with the shotgun, leaving me with seven left to go. My quick glance had shown me that at least six or seven of them were headed my way – posthaste.

One of the men crashed into the front door, finding it locked. I smiled before heading to the second floor. I crouched at the top of the landing where I could just see where the men would come in.

"It's locked! Help me kick it in!" a man screamed to one of his companions behind him.

Two loud booms shook the door frame and when the third one sounded, I heard the cracking of the jam. Then a fourth boom. The door fell flat as the wooden jam let go. One man fell onto his face as the door came in and the other almost followed suit, but his momentum kept him going and he ran right over the patch where I had kicked the wedge out of place. It was like Wile E Coyote falling into one of his own traps. It didn't even make a sound. The squared section of flooring we'd spent a day cutting out quietly fell away, dropping the man a dozen feet into the basement.

He started shrieking, yelling about his leg. The man who had fallen on his face quickly rolled to the side out of my sight and I could hear him yelling down into the hole below. He turned and fired up towards me and I ducked out of sight.

"... Is your leg broken?"

"Busted pretty bad, get me out of here!"

I peeked again when the firing had stopped. Two more men entered the doorway cautiously, their guns up and scanning. I could barely make him out, but as soon as the first one crossed the threshold I let him have it with the shotgun. The man next to him was shrouded in a pink mist as his buddy's head exploded. I had been aiming for the top of his chest so I couldn't claim any great credit there. I just got excited and hadn't been thinking straight. I pumped a fresh shell of the shotgun, took another shot. I missed, hitting the doorframe, and sending a shower of wood and splinters into the other men who been massing at the door.

"Oh shit," I yelled in a faux, afraid voice and started running up the stairs as loud as I could.

"*My rifle is human, even as I, because it is my life. Thus, I will learn it as a brother. I will learn its weaknesses, its strength, its parts, its accessories, its sights and its barrel. I will keep my rifle clean and ready, even as I am clean and ready. We will become part of each other. We will.*"

The stairs didn't go straight up. They went more into a spiral with a left-hand curve about every fifteen feet for every story level. I ran all the way up to the third level, where a plastic milk crate full of Molotov cocktails were ready to throw. These weren't your average gasoline and soap bubble cocktails. We'd taken gasoline and put chunks of Styrofoam in it, making more of a jellied napalm. To me, I thought it was a little more stable and a little safer for transport, but I wasn't going to be using them all at once.

Actually, I wanted them to follow me all the way into the building, so I could keep picking them off… if I had to blow it, so be it. By my count, there were still five men left, six, if you counted the guy who was busted up in the basement. No matter what happened, though, he wouldn't survive long anyway. Footsteps pounded up the stairs in pursuit. I got a Bic lighter out and I was ready to light one of the fuses that had been wetted with gasoline. When

I thought someone was getting close to the second landing, I heard a crash and screams and curses.

We'd pulled the carpet back on those stairs and cut through the threads. As quietly as we could, we'd pulled out the nails holding the treads in place and had replaced them with shorter nails. That way, it would take some weight - but not the weight of a couple men thumping up the stairs. At least one of them had just fallen through. Hopefully, breaking them up and slowing them down some, so that they would have to take a second to get their friends out, or that's what I was counting on.

Still, I heard more footsteps coming. I lit the fuse and I threw it. I heard angry shouts, but no screams of pain. I tore off like my ass was on fire and ran across the third floor, coming to the second apartment on my left. The devastation from the plane crash, shearing off the building was absolute and the debris crunched under my heavy footsteps. The shotgun was now in a sling over my shoulder as my hands were full of the Molotov cocktails in the plastic milk crate. From where I was now, I could see down to the front of the building, and I quickly lit the fuses on several of them and started throwing them down at the front door. They exploded, spewing flames all over. No one would be going out through the main doors anytime soon.

More angry shouts greeted the firebombs, but I had managed to thin the gang out as much as I'd wanted to. Footsteps pounded the hallway behind me and I knew that it was just a matter of seconds. I'd known that I might get trapped in this room, so that's why I had peeled away the sheet rock between this apartment and the one next to it. I'd left the door open to the apartment I was in, to give them a pretty good idea of where I'd gone. I wanted them to come in here. I took a quick look and one figure came running through the doorway. I took a snapshot and the heavy buckshot tore into the man. It wasn't a fatal wound, but it hit him low in the hip and upper leg. The man staggered and fell, but there were still more in the hallway.

Gunfire had me ducking as wood and drywall exploded next to my head. I racked another set of shells into the chamber and kept going. I ran through the abandoned apartment and into the bathroom, slamming the door. Another hole awaited me and I could already hear them trying to crash through the doors of the apartment I had just left.

It would take them just a few moments to figure out what I had just done, but hopefully they were all upstairs now and in those rooms because I ran out of the second apartment's main door and sprinted down the hallway. I grabbed one last Molotov, leaving the rest where they were, not wanting to be burdened, and lit it. I paused for a minute, turned and threw it as hard as I could towards the end of the hallway where the stairs were. It exploded against the wall, painting everything with flames.

"He's out here!" someone shouted.

I ran all the way to the end of the hallway, to the last apartment on the right. I nearly burst through the doorway. Before things had gone south, this apartment had been getting remodeled. Being on the third floor, the apartment had been gutted and a garbage chute had been affixed to the window. That was my quick escape route. I pulled the shotgun around on the drop sling, so it would be in front of me and I jumped in the tube feet first. It was like no slide I'd ever been on, and about a thousand times scarier than the water parks I'd tried over in Dubai, a million years ago in the sandbox.

I dropped three stories faster than was humanly sane. Although the chute didn't let me reach terminal velocity, I was going faster than I'd ever felt comfortable with. But the wild ride down the chute was enough to slow me down, so that when I hit the stacks of mattresses at the bottom, I didn't die. That was one last thing we'd done. We'd carried some mattresses out and lined up my landing area. The men would have to be idiots to follow me out. If they did, I could pick them off as they came out of the chute. If they started shooting from the windows, they would make themselves an easy target as well, but I wasn't going to let them get that opportunity.

If it hadn't been for the mattresses, I would have had worse than the wind knocked out of me. I would have had all of the sense knocked out of me, too. Maybe even my life knocked out of me, but they had worked. Still, it was no easy task to drag myself to my feet and use the wheel to spark the Bic lighter one last time. I knelt by a small casement window that led into the basement. We'd left a half-full drum down there and the fumes had to have been getting to the man that was lying in the basement with his leg too badly broken to move.

Again, this was something that I hadn't quite thought up entirely myself, but being in the Marines, I knew a lot more about IEDs than your average civilian or even militia member. What I was doing, though, was straight out of Timothy McVeigh's playbook. You would think in a city the size of Chicago, it would've been hard to find industrial fertilizer, but you'd be wrong. Chicago was a port city, and the Great Lakes had still been a big waterway and source for shipping. It might've been in the city, but there was farmland all over Illinois. All it had taken was two bags of the dry fertilizer, eight gallons of diesel fuel, and three and a half sticks of dynamite pushed into the mixed slurry.

I ran. I ran like hell. I ran as if my very life depended on it. I had no idea what the blast was going to do to the tunnels below, and that was why I'd made sure to tell Danielle, Jamie, Mel, and Jeremy to be at least a half a mile away from the theater entrance down below. I had no idea how quick the fuse was going to burn, but I guessed it'd been at least twenty seconds from when I'd lit the fuse. When I'd counted up to fifteen, I dove into an alleyway and wedged myself in behind a dumpster.

My DI Matroka's words haunted me, "*Before God, I swear this creed. My rifle and I are the defenders of my country. We are the masters of our enemy. We are the saviors of my life. So be it, until victory is America's and there is no enemy, but peace!*"

The explosion sounded like… like the roaring of an angry God. The noise was almost too big to even describe, as flaming debris was flung hundreds of feet into the air. I struggled for my breath, as the explosion sucked in all of the available oxygen it needed for that moment.

When the pressure wave hit half a heartbeat later, I wasn't surprised. I'd been ready, as a matter of fact. I had closed my eyes and opened my mouth. I cringed and protected my head with my arms and although several things hit the dumpster I was hiding behind, nothing hit me. I only waited ten seconds before peeking my head out and starting to run.

"We are the saviors of my life," I repeated aloud as I looked around. "Oorah," I whispered to myself and started moving.

I did a half a circle around the block until I could get the old apartment building in view. It had simply collapsed in on itself. What was left standing was on fire, and it looked like even that was starting to crumble. There was no one in pursuit – not that I'd expected anyone to be. I slung my shotgun over my shoulder and started walking towards the burning building slowly. I wasn't surprised to see the cracks in the cement a hundred yards away from the apartment building. I needed to be sure I'd gotten all of them, though, not just the ones inside the apartment building, but any left hiding the bank.

I worked my way back to my original hiding position and peeked around the corner at the bank. The only sound I could hear was the stone and brickwork falling in the fire, greedily consuming everything combustible. The bank looked quiet and dark inside. I broke cover slowly because there was no good cover around it. That was one of the good things, not *good* exactly… bad choice of words… one of the *smart* things that gang had done. They'd cleared out a field of fire around the bank. Today, it was their greed and their lust that had been their downfall.

I took the safety back off the shotgun and held it in the ready position, knowing that the next round there would be a slug. I'd let off four rounds and I briefly thought of putting four more in, but I didn't want to lose my focus. Step-by-step, my fear grew. I'd entered buildings like this before. My mind flashed back to one such a time, just briefly.

We'd been going house to house, looking for Al Qaeda fighters and had taken fire by a sniper. We'd sheltered in an old bank, not knowing that right behind the counter, there'd been three men lying in wait for us. We had walked right into their trap, right into another killing funnel. We had taken half a second to look around and started clearing the bank when they'd popped up from behind the counter, firing as they rose. We'd reacted immediately, returning fire. I lost a good friend that day and I'd never had a deep-seated urge to go banking after that. We'd sheltered in the bank until we were able to call in mortar fire to the rooftop sniper.

… But that was in Fallujah. This was just an old rundown shitty bank in Chicago. I approached the door anyway, at an oblique angle. When I didn't see anyone, I started moving into the doorway with the shotgun at the ready. Everything appeared empty, if you wanted to call the mess and debris they'd left behind empty. I'd already passed the burn barrel in the front of the building, but the inside was trashed. Discarded clothing and blankets were arranged into makeshift sleeping pallets. Empty beer and booze bottles and cans littered the floor and on the counter, was a variety of guns and ammunition.

It was a lot less than I'd hoped for, but it was a lot more than I'd expected. I just couldn't believe that they'd left it all out in the open…

I paused, suddenly real wary. This was wealth beyond means, and it was just laid out like it was on display. My first instinct had been to go over and claim it as my own, right away. This had been part of the reason I'd hit the smaller group first. To get the easy one out of the way first and then, gear up to go after the others. I carefully worked my way back to the counter where the tellers would normally walk through, looking for any tricks or traps.

Part of the counter swung up to allow entrance and before I just grabbed it and pushed it up, I looked at it. An eyelet had been screwed into the bottom and a thin black wire ran back and out of sight. I crawled on my hands and knees looking and when I saw what the black wire was attached to, I froze. Somehow, those assclowns had found a grenade and the wire was attached to the pin of it. Anyone who just opened up the swinging section would've dislodged it, and would've been blown to hell a second later.

I pulled my Leatherman out of the pouch on my belt, flipped it open and cut the wire as close as I could to the grenade. I let out a sigh of relief and pulled it loose from the duct tape. I thought about leaving it at that, but I decided if there was one trap there was bound to be more. And oh boy, was I right. The next one wasn't a tripwire. It was worse, because of what it would've done to me. If I'd missed the grenade, it would've been hard to miss the nails sticking up out of the debris on the floor. I kicked the debris aside, exposing a simple, yet effective trap. A one-by-six had been filled full of nails, their sharpened points sticking up, and then debris had been laid over the top of it. I slowed down and worked my way further, noticing that the door to the vault was already open. It wasn't opened all the way, but just enough to see the crack that was there. However, I wanted to clear the teller area first before I got into any of that.

On the back counter, where the tellers often counted out large sums of money, was a variety of trophies or trading goods. I couldn't tell which. Jewelry and personal belongings of all sorts littered the counter. Rings, necklaces, earrings, watches… anything with precious metal in it was laid out there. It took me a moment to realize what I was looking at. It was all the jewelry from their robberies or their kidnapped victims.

It still didn't answer the question that had been bothering me for a couple days now, what had they been eating? I'd already observed that other than the booze and the beer, I hadn't seen any evidence of them really bringing some sort of food in any kind of quantity inside. I decided that after one more quick look in here, I would go look inside the vault and make sure that no one was hiding out. The door looked to be at least a few hundred pounds. It wouldn't be something that could just be opened quickly, so I needed to make sure that there were no other traps waiting for me.

I was lucky. There wasn't anything else. A quick look around showed that there'd been three .45 Colts, a revolver, and an AR platform rifle laid out, with all sorts of ammunition for all different calibers. I could use those to barter and get what I really wanted. All I had to do was survive this encounter and get the hell out of here. So, there was only one place left to check. The vault.

I grabbed the handle on the vault, already feeling dread building up inside of me. This whole place smelled bad. The smell of unwashed bodies filling the small lobby of the old bank. The smell became worse as soon as I started pulling the handle back. I could smell the unmistakable funk of death. With the door fully open, I stood there for a second. I'd seen a lot of shit during my almost twenty years of fighting wars all across the world, but I'd never seen cannibalism, real cannibalism, up close.

The carcasses, for lack of a better word, had been hung from the ceiling. I could already feel it taking me back to a darker place in my mind. I saw there was nothing I wanted in the vault, so I quickly shut the door. I recognized Curtis hanging on a hook and I spit disgustedly, trying to get the foul taste of the air out of my mouth.

I noticed a small backpack sitting in a corner

near where the hand grenade had been. I walked over to it slowly, still checking for traps, and made sure it wasn't sitting on a grenade with the pin pulled. It wasn't. I picked the backpack up, felt the weight of it, and looked inside.

Three grenades with black electrical tape were waiting in the bottom, along with some rope and a knife. I took the one that I'd disarmed earlier out of my pocket and added it to the backpack. Then, I went and grabbed an old T-shirt that'd been lying in a pile on the floor to separate things out. I put each .45 pistol into the bag, wrapped part of the shirt over the revolver, and then added the ammunition. I hefted the pack over my shoulder and I could feel the straps straining from the weight. I had at least a few hundred rounds of ammunition, judging by how many boxes I'd put in, but I had no way of knowing if they'd been full or not.

Then, my eyes turned and settled on all the jewelry. If I left it behind, my conscience would be clear, but if I took it... I could use it for barter and trade. Precious metals were still a hot commodity, but not as much as food, ammunition, and medication. If I left everything here, the next person to come into the bank would find it and use it for their own purposes. I decided not to decide, so I took the backpack off and held it open. I swept all of it into the backpack. I would let the women and children decide what to do with it.

Someday, I would be leaving them to go look for my wife and daughter. This might give them the edge they needed, that extra little bit to survive.

I knew I was running tight on time and people would start to worry that the worst had happened to me. This trick had worked once, and as long as the tunnel wasn't damaged, it should work again. I was going to use the coal chute from the old theater to get back down to the family.

CHAPTER 9

By the time I got to the back utility room of the theater and had pulled the trapdoor, my back was killing me. I fished the length of rope from the bottom of the backpack and tied one end off to the backpack handles. The weight of the guns, ammo, and the jewelry would've been too much for me to go down with it, and with the grenades in there too, I didn't want to just let it slide down unattended.

Instead, I lowered it down, foot by foot, hand over hand, with the rope until it had gone the forty to fifty feet to hit the bottom. I thought about tying the rope off and using it to slow my descent because my back was killing me, but I didn't want to leave any sort of clear evidence that I'd been down here recently. So, I let the end of the rope go and crawled in.

I was able to control my descent a lot better than I'd been able to when I'd been carrying Maggie's, I mean Mel's, unconscious form. I took it slow and when I needed a break, I took it. When I got close to the end, I felt for the indented lip. It was probably someplace where they clipped the work light almost a hundred years ago. Finding it with my hands, I pulled myself out and lowered myself to the ground. I fumbled around in the darkness, patting my pockets, trying to find either the Bic lighter or the flashlight, but I couldn't find either one.

If everything had gone to plan, all of the exits would've been covered, so I wasn't surprised when a flashlight clicked on, blinding me.

"Oh, my God. Are you okay?" Mel asked me.

"If you quit blinding me, I might be."

"God, it sounded like something crashed up there, was that the bomb going off?" Mel said her face now illuminated by the backwash of the flashlight.

"Yeah, it took down most of the building and the rest of it's crumbling in on itself. You heard from any of the others yet?"

"No, I was getting ready to go look for them, to see if any of the tunnels had collapsed and cut us off. You were gone a really long time."

I winced. "I'm sorry about that. It took a little longer than I'd thought, they had some tripwires and grenades and other types of things set up. I did get some supplies though and I did get… some other stuff. Let's go find your mom and the others and get back to the main room."

* * *

We were all sitting around the campfire, Mouse half asleep in my lap. It'd been two hours since I'd gotten back into the tunnels and I was telling the less gory details to the assembled group of kids. Many of them smiled, a couple cheered, but when I started pulling out the watches, the earrings, the rings, all of the loot that'd been begotten by pain, everyone fell silent.

"Danielle and Jeremy, this I wanted to leave up to you guys… The gang members had all of this loot, but I don't think there's gonna be much of a chance of finding who it belongs to. I know that at some point, I'm gonna be leaving the tunnel system to go find my family. You could use this, trade with it topside. Some kind of a stash. I'll be sure to leave you guys some of the guns and ammunition, too." For a second, they just looked at each other and then they looked at me and I looked at the pile. I'd expected Jeremy to be the one to object, but I' was wrong.

"How many do you think this is?" Danielle asked me.

"I have no way of knowing, kid… too many."

"We have no way of knowing that this even came from victims," Jeremy said. "They could've been going house to house searching through stuff, too. I know before I took up with Dick here, I was doing much of the same. I mean, the people were either dead or gone or headed off to a FEMA camp somewhere."

"You know," Jamie said piping up, "he's got a point there. You don't know where this stuff came from. That might mean the difference of getting enough medication for one of the kids, or food when the trap lines aren't producing. Or more shells for the guns. I don't think there's a moral high ground here in regards to the loot."

"Do you guys recognize any of this stuff, I mean, is any of it yours from… before?" Mel asked the group.

Danielle used her hands and spread everything out so that no one single piece was covering another and everyone crowded around and took a quick peek at it. One by one, they shook their heads and walked away, giving room for the other kids to see. Even the little kids, including Mouse, went and looked through everything solemnly.

"I've always wanted to get my ears pierced," Mouse said. "Do you think Miss Salina would let me get my ears pierced and I could have a pair of earrings?"

"I don't know, sweetie," I told her, picking her up, "but right now, you don't need a hole in your head," I told her grinning.

"I don't have a hole in my head…" she said feeling all over her scalp.

I smiled.

"Hey, what about the guys you got in the street?" Danielle asked.

I hadn't thought of that. They had been carrying guns and potential supplies. I had been so keyed up and ready to roll that I'd forgotten about them and whatever it was they'd dropped. No one was still alive when I'd walked through there, that I did remember.

"Uh, to be honest, I forgot about them. When I started running after lighting the fuse, I was more worried about not getting my head blown off by flying debris… and when I'd made sure the bank was cleared, I got out of there a different way. It could all still be there…"

My words choked off when Jeremy walked up with a bundle made out of a sweater. He opened it. It was another AK-47 style rifle and two pistols.

"You weren't supposed to come topside!" I was pissed, how could he have done this? I mean, I'd been counting on him to take care of everyone if or when I wasn't around…

"You needed someone to have your back," Jeremy said. "You never saw me. I got the stuff and left before anyone in the area came to see what went down."

"Of all of the stupid, thoughtless…"

"Stop, Uncle Dick," Mouse said, pulling out the hairbrush.

I swear she kept that in her pocket for occasions just like this. She held up her hands and I swooped her up and held her close to me. She laid her small head on my shoulder with her hands around my neck.

"I can always brush your hair if it would make you feel better."

We all busted up at that. It was just too funny.

"I'd love to see that!" Mel said, and Danielle

nodded, poking her in the ribs.

"I wonder what the Devil Dog looks like with his hair cut?" Jeremy asked.

I stopped laughing. "You know what, that's a great idea. Losing the beard really threw them off... I mean..."

"I can do it when you're ready," Jamie said. "I used to be a hair stylist a long time ago."

"That might work," I admitted. "Give me half a second, maybe walk up on them..."

"Where's the next big gang?" Pauly asked me.

"You remember where I found you and Mouse?" I asked him.

The little boy shuddered and shook his head. I regretted answering him at once. Apparently, he still carried the memories as vividly as his sister did. It had been thoughtless of me. Dammit.

"Yeah, the museum where the bad men are," Mouse answered from my arms.

"How many?" Jeremy asked.

"It's a big group. It's going to take a lot of watching to set them up. In the meantime, we have to make sure we stay on top of everything else we have to do. We can't just do another trap house with this gang. There's way too many of them."

"Just blow them up," Mouse said, and I put her down so I could look her in the eyes.

"I blew up the guys that hurt you two already. I'm going to get the rest, though, don't you worry. You're too little to worry about mean stuff like that."

"So, tell me about the museum," Danielle said and Jeremy, Jamie, and Mel nodded as well.

* * *

The ground level was split up into a ton of extra exhibits. Danielle had busted into a boarded up gas station that had already been ransacked and picked up a couple of the brochures that they'd had around the city. I was mildly shocked to see that there was a floor plan on it, with a description of what was where. For a place to take over, the museum looked like it'd be a hard nut to crack, to be honest. It was built of stone, with large columns facing the entrances. Inside, there were three levels. Depending on how much they had done with the interior, there wouldn't be a ton of tactical terrain when first entering. So I had to come up with a plan or a distraction…

And no, I didn't want to use Danielle as bait again. She had a cut on her foot to show for it, and I was uncomfortable with how Jeremy had reacted after she'd come back. He was beside himself and I had to decide whether to act the proud father figure for Jeremy, or the angry father figure protecting his daughter. It left me all kinds of conflicted… But perhaps they could still do something to help with the distraction.

"Jeremy, what about the truck?" I asked him.

"What truck?" he looked at me puzzled.

"When I shot up those guys… was the old pickup truck still there in the middle of the stalled cars, or…?"

"I don't remember, to be honest," he said, "but I can go check while I'm out there tonight."

"I told you," I said. "I can do it. The market people know me."

I fumed, he'd been angling to get out more and I'd stopped it, citing the dangers and his responsibilities.

"So how am I going to meet the right people if I never get to go? I mean, you're not exactly planning on staying in Chicago forever."

Dammit again, he was right.

"You can't be seen with me, though. Too many people are gunning for me."

"You ever stop to think that maybe we should be gunning for them? Make them wonder and worry themselves?" Jeremy was defiant and Danielle, still looking fresh and neat, nodded.

"I'd go too, but I think I'd cause more issues than you would, Dick," she said.

"Yeah, it isn't a safe place for women and children lately. It's like every asshole in the world is topside, with only a handful that are honest, decent folks."

"So," Jeremy said, "We need a couple more things. We're out of canned goods, salt, seasonings. Unless you like your baked rat souffle without the special dry rub..." he let his words trail off, and I grinned.

"None of us want to eat like this," I told him.

"I know, but it makes it taste better, doesn't it?"

I sighed. I knew that. I knew that we'd have to do something, and there was only so much I could carry myself, and I could only tempt fate so many times a week.

"Ok. Dammit, ok. You come with me to the market, and we'll swing by and see if that old truck is still sitting there."

"Why wouldn't it be?" he asked.

"I don't know if the gang moved it or left it. They strung up the guys I'd killed and..."

I broke off, a wet burp almost gagging me as I fought my gorge down. The men I'd killed had been hanging up like a side of beef inside the vault of the bank.

"We'll check it out. It'll be good to see who's around, checking on the bank," I told them all.

"What do you need us to do?" Pauly asked.

"I need you little ones to help Miss Danielle as much as she needs it. Find as much wood in the storm drains as you can, and work on your reading."

"I don't like reading," Mouse mumbled. "I like the picture books and board games."

"Tell you what," I said, "How about we reward you kids with an equal amount of time? One hour of reading for one hour of games or stories?" I asked them.

They cheered, their joyful voices echoed in the dank subterranean chamber.

"Can you shoot?" I asked Jeremy, who was grinning ear to ear about being able to join me topside.

"I was in the ROTC, planning on enlisting this fall," Jeremy said, picking up the AK-47 and working the charging bolt.

"You any good with that?" I asked him.

"I qualified as a marksman at an NRA range.

My dad taught me how to shoot before..." his words trailed off and I nodded. Before was a heavy subject, not one we all liked to talk about much.

"How many mags you have?" I asked him.

"Found two spares on the man you shot in the street and the one that was in the gun from inside the bank. Four twenty round mags. Only two of them had any ammo in, but I think I have enough loose rounds to fill them all up."

"What about a pistol?" I asked him.

"I've shot a 1911 .45, my dad had one..."

I pointed to the pile. I already carried one, but hardly ever used it. I'd gotten spoiled by my shotgun and although I could shoot anything, and shoot it well, the KSG was fast becoming my security blanket.

"Take one of the .45s and all the spare mags you can find. If we're going to do this, let's get enough supplies between the two of us that we won't have to go back topside until we're ready to hit the gang in the museum."

"You got it," Jeremy said grinning.

"I want to go, too," Jamie said. "I need to get some stuff... for me and Mel."

"No! No way. That's out of the question," I told her indignantly.

As it turned out, I was wrong.

CHAPTER 10

"Why do they have the market set up in the middle of an intersection?" Jamie asked me.

She'd covered her hair with a stocking cap and wore a large plaid shirt of mine to hide her figure. Her curves still showed through, giving away the fact that she was a lady, but it dulled the feminine effect she had when guys first saw her. Not that I trusted everyone inside the market, but it would make life a little easier. Hell, it would've made life a lot easier if she'd have just stayed home. Instead, she'd gotten indignant, then angry, and in the end, she told me she would go and there was nothing I could say or do to stop her.

Since she wasn't a prisoner and I didn't want to set a horrible precedent, I had to do the right thing.

I did what men all over the world have done when confronted with a woman who had her mind made up. Yup, I gave in.

"They use the cars to restrict movement in or out through one entrance. From inside, they can see down the four streets and there's a few guys who are paid in food to watch for any approaching trouble. They may not recognize me with my beard shaved off, though," I told her.

She looked at me and smiled, "You're doing nothing to keep it smooth, though, it's already growing back."

True, I hadn't shaved since that first day. Still, not having half a chest full of beard would throw off a lot of people. Hell, I couldn't remember if Salina had ever seen me without that beard. Time was funny for me like that, when you quit caring about things, about perceptions of others. You just existed. You survived. The days now began to be measured by how much food you could eat, waking up without pain… It was a struggle.

"Yeah, I know," I told her. "I don't want to stand out too much. Most people don't shave topside anymore. Sometimes, they knock the fuzz back with scissors, but disposable razors aren't being made anymore. But you can sharpen scissors."

"That's true. What do you think about Jeremy? Do you think he got in already?"

"Yeah, I think so. I told him what to say to Luis. Jeremy was right, he's not some little kid anymore. I feel kind of bad for treating him like one."

"You're doing the best you can for these kids,"

Jamie said. "The only reason I needed to come up was I was slowly going crazy. I'm... claustrophobic," she admitted after a moment.

"So being down there..."

"Is like a slow kind of agony."

"So, you don't think it's selfish of me to want to leave and find my family when I'm done here?" I asked her.

She considered that for a minute or two.

"Maybe, in the traditional sense, but is that a bad thing? To want to be with your loved ones? I don't think so... I mean, you said you were going to talk to Doctor Salina about Mouse and Pauly..."

"Yeah, I can't take them with me. As much as I like the rascals, they aren't mine and I can't be the parent they'd need me to be. That hurts to admit, so don't spread that shit around."

"Don't worry, Dick," she said. "Most people probably already have you figured out anyways."

"Eh? How's that?" I asked her.

"Just in everything you do. In how you talk to people, how you act. You're a dangerous man with a soft touch. A warrior who is forcing himself to be a nurturer. It's admirable, but you're trying to be all things at once. It's going to slowly drive you crazy if you don't start living your own life..."

Her words cut off at a hiss as she realized what she'd said, but I chuckled softly and pulled her into a quick one armed hug and let her go. As far as females went, she was a good one. If I wasn't already spoken for in my heart, I might have even been interested... But she was spoken for too and neither of us was interested. Platonic friends for now.

"Looks like there's some kind of commotion inside. Let's go," I told her.

I'd looked up and gotten a glimpse of a large throng of people in the middle of the intersection a couple blocks ahead. We were close enough now to see over or through the side windows of the cars. Some kind of scuffle was going on. We broke into a jog and Luis stepped in front of the opening with his gun coming up.

"Hold on there, you two. You can't just..."

"Luis, dammit, what's going on?" I barked.

His face screwed up in thought for a moment and then his eyes widened in understanding.

"Dick? Oh, wow, man, uh... new guy came in. Somebody tried to pickpocket him. The guards are trying to break it up. Probably going to toss both of them..."

"Later," I said pushing past him, reaching back and grabbing onto Jamie's wrist and dragged her along behind me.

My right hand was free, and I didn't want to use the scattergun in such close quarters with a ton of people. Instead, I pulled out my single stack Colt 1911 in .45, same as some of the other guns we'd found. I let go of her wrist and considered the crowd of people. There were at least twenty men and a couple of ladies circling and cheering what was happening in the middle. It was like a boxing match I'd seen years ago. The way the crowd was acting... I knew it had to have been Jeremy, and I could see a couple of the guards in the middle struggling to pull apart two men.

"Get out the way," I bellowed, but nobody paid attention.

I pulled one man nearly off his feet and shoved another out of the way as I got close. The man I'd shoved shouted something at me, and when I saw a gleam of metal, I turned catching his wrist, as close to twelve inches of steel headed towards my chest. I used a wrist lock while still holding the .45 in my right hand and pulled his overextended arm across my shoulder as I turned and pulled down. His wrist shattered with a wet crunch and the blade hit the pavement. He started screaming and that, more than anything else, was what made the people pause and look. I held up my right hand and fired off a round into the air for effect. People paused and several reached for their firearms. I ignored them when I saw that Jeremy was on the ground, both of his hands trying to pull away the hands and arms of an older man who was sitting on top of his chest, choking him.

I was still wearing an old beat up pair of combat boots and they weren't known for comfort. What they were known for was doing the job, durability, and leaving really funny marks in the sides of people's faces when you dropkicked them. The boot connected with a thud to the side of the man's temple. He fell over sideways, his hands releasing his choke hold on Jeremy. I heard Jeremy start gasping for breath and I followed my kick to the head up by jumping over the kid and landing another one into the soft of the man's sunken stomach.

"The..." the air whooshed out of him and I holstered my .45. I reached down and grabbed Jeremy by the front of his shirt and started yanking him up.

My blood was up. I was pissed off and if people didn't quit pointing their guns at me...

"The fuck's the matter with you?" I screamed at half of them.

I reached for the KSG on the drop sling. Standing, it almost tucked itself neatly into the space between my right arm and my body. Seeing it and hearing my voice made a couple of them flinch and that gave me an extra half moment.

"You don't get those guns off of me, I'm going through you next!" I threatened, pointing to a young man who had a Saturday night special pointed my way.

He didn't quite drop the pistol so much as fumbled his quick put away.

"Dick?" One of the guards asked, who was picking up the man I'd kicked, my boot having left an imprint on his stupid face.

"Yeah, what of it? If you and your friends don't lower your guns, you better make sure you kill me straight off, or I'm going to hunt every one of you fuckers down later."

I realized that I wasn't just bluffing this time. I was enraged. Pissed. When one of the guards moved towards Jeremy and started pulling his arms behind his back, I swung the butt of the KSG at him, hitting him in the chest and knocking him back. He went for his .45 and I kicked his hand as it was clearing his holster. The gun went off, the shot hitting the pavement and throwing up chunks, but he'd dropped the gun. People dropped down to scramble for it and I pulled the kid closer to me.

He was getting his breath back, but he had both hands covering his throat. Already I could see the bruises forming.

"I said guns down, or a lot of people are going to die. Right now."

I had the pump shotgun in a two handed grip and waited for somebody to move. Nobody put their guns on the ground, but they all lowered them. The guard kneed a scrawny man in the chest who'd been trying to get the pistol that he'd dropped and turned to face me angrily.

"Dick, what the ever-loving fuck do you think you're doing?" the guard snarled.

I couldn't remember him or place his face, but he was familiar.

"You come after one of mine, you can expect to die, badly," I said to him.

The guard squinted and then looked at Jeremy. This was not how I had wanted this to go. I hadn't wanted him to be connected to me until after I had left the area. Dammit, this was why I hadn't wanted him to come topside.

"I just wanted a round. A single round. The kid has four full magazines," the man I'd kicked said, almost weeping.

"So you did what? Tried to take it, take a mag? Then you tried to kill him when he fought back?" I snarled, moving on the guard who held the man, despite the man trying to back up.

"I just wanted a round! Little fucker wouldn't give me one."

"I should have just shot you," I told him.

"Hey, Dick. You know the rules, man," Luis said walking up.

People parted for him in a way they hadn't for me. They knew that when he left his spot, shit had gotten heavy.

"Yeah. Thieves are shot," I said, looking at the man who was now trembling.

"And we don't allow violence in the market. You've been warned before. Get your kid and..."

"Don't," Jamie said, pulling the stocking hat off her head, letting her hair fall down in cascading sheets of raven colored tresses.

"Excuse me?" He turned and then stammered as Jamie crossed her arms over the baggy shirt, showing off her curves.

"I said, don't. The kid is with us," Jamie said, looking at me. "He didn't start this by the look of it, and you were too busy watching from the front. It's like you were getting off on watching it."

Luis flushed a bit and a couple of the guards looked at their boots.

"I know there isn't any more TV, but you can't allow a boxing match to happen and then throw everyone out afterward. The kid was going to be choked out and only two of you were half-heartedly stopping it. The rest of you were cheering them on. What kind of fucked up town is this? Dick said you were supposed to be the good guys?"

She wasn't quite screaming at the end, but her

voice was projecting so loudly and so clearly that everyone in the market had fallen silent, except for the man with a broken wrist, who was still crying out.

"You ok, kid?" I asked Jeremy, who was feeling his pockets with one hand and pulling the AR loose from the sling to check it out and make sure the tumble hadn't damaged it.

"Yeah," he said in a rasp, "Caught the fucker with his hand inside my pocket. Told him to..." he coughed and then spit, "Told him no. He pulled a knife. Didn't feel like killing him, so I thought I'd…"

"Get your ass kicked," I told him. "Kid, you don't ever go hand to hand in a knife fight."

"Isn't that what you kinda did?" Jamie asked me.

Luis had a hard time taking his eyes off of her, but when he did, he turned to look at the man who was curled up on the ground rocking back and forth, holding his hand to his chest, and then back to me.

"I had a gun," I told her. "I didn't think the dumb-ass had enough brain matter to stop a slug at close range and didn't want to hurt the rest of them. Besides, I've trained for this, it's different."

"You done playing around, Dick?" A loud, clear voice came out from the crowd and I turned to see Salina.

"I don't play games," I said in a low voice.

"You're playing one now. Junkyard devil dog. It's how you be. Only way you feel comfortable is to be the meanest son of a bitch on the playground."

Her words were harsh, but they were true. I often let the baser side of me out in situations like this and I took a deep cleansing breath.

"Salina, I have no quarrel with you," I told her. "And, as far as this guy goes," I said, lowering the shotgun and pointing at the thief with my left hand, "Maybe it's his first time. Shoot him or not, but I'm not wasting a shell on him."

The man almost collapsed and the guard let him fall instead of holding his weight up.

"Dick, you can't come in here and start manhandling people," Luis told me. "We have rules…"

"And you let the fight go on for your amusement. I did what you should have done. Throw me out, who gives a shit? When the people here see that you're no better than the rest of the gangs running loose, using people for fun and amusement… they'll quit coming here and you'll lose your meal ticket."

My words had a chilling effect on him and the people who'd been talking quietly. Vendors and shoppers alike went silent and nodded.

"It won't happen again. Agreed?" Luis asked.

I knew he was both saying he wouldn't allow it to happen on his watch again, and asking me to not put him in a position where I had to hurt his vendors or customers. So be it.

"Agreed."

"Ok everyone, break it up," Luis growled.

We waited a few moments as people started to disperse. The man who had slumped on the ground was spat on by several people, many hurling insults at him, telling him they'd be watching out for him.

"You new here?" I asked, watching all this happen impassively.

"Fu—" he rolled over and retched.

Must have kicked him in the stomach good or given him a concussion. Damn.

"Yeah, fuck you too, asshole," I said.

"Dick…" Jamie's voice was quiet, somewhere behind me.

"Come on, lady. Let's go see the doc," I told her, then turned to Jeremy, "Come on, kid. I'm going to have her check out your throat."

* * *

"I would have had Jerome break it up if I'd known it was one of your kids," Salina said to us.

We'd sat down in the plastic lawn chairs that she had at her folding table with her doctoring supplies. Jerome glowered from behind her, standing watch.

"You should have, regardless of who it was. My kids, your kids…"

"And what if he got a knife in the stomach for some random strangers? Who would take care of his family? Me? Who would work with me and make sure the junkies didn't rob me?" Salina said.

I didn't know if that was a dig at me or not, so I chose to ignore it.

"When you decide to do nothing, you're no better than the people who hide with their heads up their asses and let the atrocities happen around you." I wasn't quite snarling, trying to keep my anger in check.

Why was I so angry? That I couldn't figure out—

"Dick, calm down," Jamie said, and a cool hand started massaging the back of my neck.

I almost fell over backward in surprise, but she leaned in close to me and kissed me on the forehead. My eyes did not quite bug out, but it was a close thing. Salina chuckled.

"Not everyone is you," Doc said with an arched eyebrow, "and I'm guessing that you've been holding out on me. You found Mary?" she asked, surprised.

I couldn't speak. What the hell??

Jamie spoke up. "No, I just sort of… I mean, he saved me and my daughter a while back and I kinda think this big guy is too hard on himself."

She wrapped her arms around me, and I could feel the swell of her breasts pushing into my back. Despite my panic, I could feel my body starting to respond. What was she doing?

"Oh, ok then. How is little Mouse doing?" Salina asked me.

Jamie let go, giving me air to breathe again. She didn't answer, I couldn't, but it was Jeremy who did, with a raspy, phlegmy sounding voice.

"She's good. She still wants you to come visit her. I promised her that I'd introduce her and Pauly to you and Jerome sometime. She's still kind of scared of topside."

"Topside, downstairs, you guys are too much. Now let me see that neck of yours."

While she leaned over and started checking

out his neck, I stood and turned to face Jamie. The trembling had started in my arms and I put my hands in my pocket, so she wouldn't see how far off game she'd thrown me.

"What was that?" I whispered.

"I thought if they thought I was with you, I'd be a little safer... plus it'd give them a reason to understand why you almost killed a ton of people. If you had a girlfriend and one of your kids with you, I mean... I'm sorry. I didn't mean to make things worse," she whispered back quietly.

"It's been close to six years since I've been that close to a woman," I told her. "So give me a little more warning, ok?" I was going for levity, but the side of her mouth quirked up into a half a smile.

"Hearing that I had that effect on you, makes a girl feel all special-like." She grinned.

"Your husband must have his hands full with you two ladies," I said and sat down.

After a moment, she finally took the empty chair next to me.

"It's just going to bruise," Salina told him and then looked at me to see if I was paying attention.

"What about the guy with the wrist?" I asked her.

"He doesn't have any money," she said coldly, "No ammo, no precious metals and frankly, he shouldn't have been trying to stab somebody looking to break up a fight. It's the guards' jobs to do that, no matter what you think of the rest of us."

I grunted.

"What's going to happen to him?" I asked her.

"It'll heal badly, maybe get some sort of infection. Maybe lose the use of the hand, or die."

Her words were cold, and I almost made a snide remark about her Hippocratic oath, but I wasn't the one to cast stones. I'd done worse. I'd been worse. I just shrugged.

"How much for you to set it and cast it?" I asked her.

"Who's paying?" she asked me, arching an eyebrow again.

Being stuck between two beautiful women who were looking at me funny was making me all kinds of uncomfortable, especially with the way Salina's eyes kept checking out my mostly weed-whacked features. Sure, my hair was still long and in a ponytail, but the beard was down to barely a short stubble.

"Depends on the deal. I don't want to leave the kid with a ton of hard feelings when I eventually leave. I hadn't planned on outing him as one of mine," I admitted.

"Uh huh, use that excuse," Jamie teased.

"What?" I asked her, a little annoyed.

"You're not just doing it for Jeremy," she said, leaning forward to look at him and make sure he was paying attention. "You're doing it to reinforce right from wrong, so when you leave, the kid can step in."

"Well, shit..." I muttered, and Jerome chuckled.

His voice sounded like two boulders rubbing together, and not happy ones. Still, it was surprising.

"He'll do fine. You've had him for months now, teaching."

"A couple," I admitted. "So how much?" I asked Salina turning to face her again.

"You talk to Mouse for me, tell her the day after tomorrow, and you just pay for the bandages…It'll cost you two .38 shells."

Huh. I fished around in my pockets for the small bags of ammo I'd kept for trade. I found two of the older .38 S&W shells, not quite a .38 special, but they would work in the newer guns. I handed them over. Salina looked at them, nodded and pocketed them.

"What else are you looking for?" she asked me.

"Information," I whispered.

"Aren't you always…."

* * *

"I don't see a pickup… wait… is that it?" Jeremy asked me.

We'd walked back towards the old bank and had just reached the intersection where I'd saved the ladies. Jamie was still with us, but she'd tucked her hair away again and had kept her shirt loose. Twice today, I'd seen what she could do to men just by… my skin broke out into gooseflesh. First, Danielle had dressed up as bait and then Jamie had subdued Luis and I both, just by being women. As amusing as that was, I was worried what my Maggie was having to do, or not do to survive. I felt a pang in my chest, but I looked to see where Jeremy had been pointing.

In an alleyway two blocks from the bank, near the now crumpled apartment building was the pickup truck. The windshield was gone and a large chunk of brickwork had dented the hood. Still, it was the same one. Someone had taken the time to move it and change the tires I'd blown out. They'd probably taken them from one of a hundred stalled vehicles sitting dormant in the city.

"Yeah, that's it," I said.

"Am I the only one who isn't excited about the truck?" Jamie asked.

"Yeah, I know," I told her. "But I plan on using this thing to create a diversion. I'm not going to cross the country in it. It'd make us too much of a target if we're traveling alone."

"Good, because I don't know if I could handle getting in that thing."

"I just want to see if it fires up. We can roll a dumpster in front of it if we need to. Cover it up until we need to use it."

"If we can even find the keys to it..." Jeremy said, his voice still rasping.

"If the battery is any good still, I can hot-wire it."

We stood before it, but the driver's side door was so close to a building that I couldn't climb in. Instead, I climbed up onto the hood and went in through the broken-out windshield. I was careful not to cut myself on the safety glass that was shattered into chunks. Bricks must have shattered the windshield when I'd dropped the apartment building. The front of the truck seemed to have got the brunt of it. I moved a couple of bricks out of the way, got into the driver's seat and felt around. No keys in the ignition but several wires hung down below. I felt for them and then cursed. I pulled out my penlight and rolled to my right and clicked it on, so I had enough light to see what I was doing.

The wires that were hanging down had been stripped. I put two of them together and twisted them. The third I touched to it until the starter wheezed and then the motor caught. I was surprised, but it sounded like the motor was running with a halfway decent muffler. Still, it was too loud. I pulled the two wires apart, killing the motor, and carefully pushed the exposed ignition wires under the dash, in case someone had heard and came around to investigate.

"So it's good," Jeremy said as I started pulling myself out.

"Yeah," I told him, "As long as the tires hold air, I think this will work well."

"I wonder why they didn't have any food?" Jeremy asked.

I almost paused when I was crawling out, but I decided to level with him, seeing as we didn't have little ears around.

"They were cannibals. The guys I'd killed when I got Jamie and Mel loose were hanging up in the vault."

Jamie let out a retching sound and turned towards the wall. Jeremy didn't look a whole lot better.

"That's sick," he said.

"Do you remember how hungry you were when you followed me, even though you knew I would probably kill you?" I asked him.

"Yeah, but I mean..."

"I know Jeremy, it's not normal. Even on our worst day, I don't think any of us could do it. That's why it's sickening... but these guys... They weren't starving. I'm kind of worried that this has been going on elsewhere. More than just this instance."

"I... That's bad," Jamie said quietly. "If food is almost impossible to find in the city, why haven't you guys moved out of it?"

"Well, for a while, Mouse was sick," I told her. "Then I found the twins. If I hadn't been taking care of them, who would? I know Salina wants to help, but she can only afford a couple mouths, not all of the kids, you know?" I asked her.

"I think you're using that as a crutch," Jamie said. "You're pretty resourceful. You haven't been run out yet."

"Damned right he hasn't," Jeremy said grinning. "Nobody runs Dickhead out of town."

I hated this conversation. It was one I'd had a dozen times. It was the gangs, it was the kids, it was waiting for them to get better... all of those were the reasons, but none of them were. At the heart of it, was just that I was a broken man. Waiting on life to kick me down again. I'd always sort of realized it, but it had never hit home until now.

"Less talk, more work," I said, trying to change the subject.

CHAPTER 11

I'd already scoped out the gang and had hit them before. Usually before or after they had come out of the museum, never while they were in it. As far as I could tell, this group had been a Chicago street gang before the EMP event knocked out the power. They were an equal opportunity employer and I'd bought my junk from one of their guys a year or more ago.

Getting hooked isn't always a conscious decision. I'd be willing to take the blame for being weak... But when I'd arrived home from my last deployment all busted up... I'd been given an almost limitless supply of Vicodin. From there, it seemed like the pain would never go away. I never knew if the pain was real because I didn't feel it anymore. So, was it a trick of the mind back then?

When the Vicodin ran dry, I used to be able to find morphine. That was expensive stuff and it wasn't a long hop, skip, and a jump from morphine to the cheaper and more dangerous heroin. I'd just found Salina's clinic and had gone to a couple of checkups when she'd noticed the tracks on the inside of my arm. She'd known what it'd meant, what the score was.

She didn't judge me, but she didn't pity me either. That woman sat me down and gave me some hard truths. Sure, I was pissed... but when I'd realized that my life was no longer mine to control, I'd gone to her to help me kick it. Since the EMP, it was almost impossible to find anything. Score one for world annihilation, eh?

"What you got?" Danielle asked me.

She startled me. I thought I was the only one on the rooftop. She was supposed to be my lookout down below, and not even from this building!

"Jeremy came and relieved me. Jamie is watching the kids for now."

"Jeremy came to relieve you or join you?" I asked her, returning my gaze into the binoculars and glassing the museum.

"I don't know," she said, but she was smiling. I could hear it in her voice. She was smug and happy. "And he brought some more ibuprofen for you. Said being up here all crouched funny would make your back act up."

Damn the kid for being right... but still...

"Thanks."

I took the pills, popped them into my mouth

with my left hand and started feeling for the water jug I knew was beside me. My entire focus was on the entrance of the museum because I'd seen a ton of movement. Someone was coming or they were fixing to go. Seeing the rag-tag collection of old cars and trucks parked on the east side I could only guess, but if I were pressed, I'd say they were fixing to go somewhere.

"He also said you might want this, instead of your shotgun," Danielle took the AK-47 off her shoulder and laid it against the two-feet high knee wall on the flat roof. The barrel stuck up, but not by much and from a distance, it'd be impossible to tell what it was without binoculars.

"Thanks. That might come in handy," I told her. "Now scoot before Jeremy breaks cover to come find you."

"Sir, yes sir," she whispered and took off before I could swat her.

My position was a good three hundred yards away from the museum, and finding a way inside their territory hadn't been horrible. I'd gone in through the storm drains and come up through a manhole in an adjacent alleyway. The hardest part of the job had been getting the manhole up and out of place without making a ton of noise. It'd been heavy and not something you could just pick up and put down lightly.

More movement caught my eye and I focused again. Four men or what I assumed to be men, dragged out a figure who'd had their arms zip-tied together. I tensed and focused on the figure... mentally cursing myself for not having shot the AK yet. If it was a decent gun, three hundred yards would be nothing. If it was some cheap knockoff, it might not be worth the metal it was stamped and milled from.

The figure was lean and as far as I could tell, male. At least, when people are that gaunt and thin with no curves showing and you assume male. Or I do. A black sackcloth had been placed over the figure's head and he was being guided to an old Volkswagen microbus. The blue and white hippy van fired up and three of the men held their guns on the prisoner and climbed in after him. The driver goosed the gas pedal a couple of times.

Even well muffled, it was almost as loud as the hoots and jeers from the men who were left behind. I tried to bring my focus in on the hooded prisoner more when the bag was torn from his head, so one of the men could throw a punch. Even from here, I recognized the man, or at least who he resembled.

Mid-forties. Brown hair gone salt and pepper, length to mid-back. Long beard. Slimmer than me, but from a distance he looked enough like me that I was surprised.

"Damn," I muttered.

* * *

"Uncle Dick, can you tell us a story tonight?" Mouse said, plopping in my lap and holding up a hairbrush.

"I... I don't know," I said, my voice shaking a

little bit.

"You know, if they snatched him, it isn't your fault," Mel told me. "You don't know if it's because he looked like you."

"No, I don't."

"But even if they did, pretty soon all guys are going to look like you. If you hadn't noticed, not many people are shaving nowadays," Danielle said.

I nodded to her, conceding the point. I started brushing Mouse's hair. Pauly had come up and handed us bowls of the thick soup. I thanked him and put the brush down next to Mouse and started eating as she got up to eat.

"How many new ones did you count today?" Jeremy asked.

"I saw a few more men than I had before. I think they're recruiting," I admitted.

Even the gangs hadn't been immune to the starvation and die-offs. I'd seen these guys bringing stuff in and out of the museum. Buckets and buckets of stuff. What I really wanted to do, before I staged anything, was to grab one of the men and sweat the information out of him. I hadn't told the kids this, but tonight wouldn't be a night where I woke them up from my nightmares. I was going to nap, but I'd found in the pile of jewelry and junk, a wind-up camp alarm clock. I was going to sleep with that inside my pillow and hope for the best.

"How are you going to take care of so many?" Danielle asked me, sitting down next to Jamie, followed by Jeremy, and then half the kids scooted closer.

Danielle had a vested interest in seeing the guys go down. Mouse and Pauly too. It had been this gang that I'd rescued the young kids from, and if word had gone out that one of the other slaver gangs had been hit, they would probably assume it was me who had done it.

"I'll figure something out," was all I told them.

We ate in near silence and Steve, one of the twins pulled out a tattered book after we'd all finished. *Where the Wild Things Are...* I loved that book. I used to read it to Maggie when she was a kid. Instead of hurting, I held onto that memory and I felt halfway alright with the world.

* * *

It felt like I'd never slept, but when the alarm started going off, I shot my hand under the pillow and hit the button. I could hear a couple of snores cut off and the changes in breathing, but nothing that would signal I'd woken any of them up. Even at my home base, I was playing the game, so I didn't want to rock the boat for now. I got out and padded down the passageway towards the bathroom. Then, I quietly grabbed my shotgun and a dark hooded sweater and headed towards the museum. I wasn't going to go in as close as my lookout spot. The gang was more active at night, but I was hoping that they'd be lulled by the three am time and be half drunk as well.

Only the gangs had limitless supplies, it seemed. They could trade people for whatever they wanted.

It was a new kind of currency, one that I was hoping to put an end to. Human trafficking had been going on for as long as men had walked the earth. That didn't make it right, though, and I was fixing my sights on one of the largest groups out there. One that hopefully would lead me to the sick fucks by the docks.

"You'd better come back in one piece," a quiet voice came out of the darkness as I started to climb the staircase to a sub-basement that hooked into an old building.

I spun, the shotgun coming up, and I found Danielle in my flashlight's beam. My heart was going a thousand beats a second and I dropped the gun, letting it tuck itself back in place on the drop sling.

"I will," I told her. "I was trying to sneak out."

"I know," Danielle said, "that's what woke me up. When you go take a leak in the middle of the night, you stomp around like a damned dinosaur. You were stealthy tonight."

Was that even a thing?

"Kid, I promise I'll come back in one piece."

"You need backup?"

I looked at her, and her eyes were large. I knew it was personal for her, and I considered the pros and cons of letting her come with me.

"Not this time," I told her, "but if I get a chance to snag one of these guys, want to help me question him?" I asked.

She nodded quickly.

"You want to wait here for me?" I asked her,

"I'm going to try to snag someone. I might need a hand dragging them if my back acts up."

I could see her teeth in the dark and she nodded again.

* * *

I went up through an old building's sub-basement. The sub-basement had been sealed off at least once, but it was in an old firehouse that had been renovated into flat-style apartments. I was able to squeeze my way to the basement by crawling up along the wall where the sewer lines came down. The support bracing was like stairs... and what used to be the opening for the coal chute was boarded over. I made quick work of that with a pry bar, trying to be as quiet as I could.

Nothing stirred above me, except for the stealthy rustle that told me that rats were nearby. That was nothing strange, to be honest. The city hadn't kept up on the poisoning and for a while, their population numbers had exploded. I'd worried what they might be contracting or passing on, but in the end, it didn't matter much. I got the final board out and I climbed up and into the basement level.

I clicked on the flashlight and looked around, one hand on the pistol grip of the shotgun just in case. Boxes and garbage bags of stuff were all over. On one side, an old boiler sat quiet and cold, water pipes coming out of the manifold and shooting up into the spaces above it. In another time, the copper wiring and plumbing would have been ripped out of an abandoned building, but now copper was almost useless. So there it sat.

I thought about using the stairs, but I saw large basement windows, the kind that swung up and out on one wall. As quiet as I could, trying not to trip over the garbage and boxes that littered the floor, I tried to peer out. The flashlight just reflected the light back into my eyes. I knew better, but I was getting anxious. I clicked it off and sat in the darkness to let my eyes adjust.

It took a while, but soon I could make out a difference in the gloom. Moonlight filtered through the windows. Weak, but I could start to make things out. I couldn't quite get to the latch, so I turned and saw an old kitchen chair under the stairs. As carefully as I could, I got it and came back, releasing the latch and pushing the window open. It squeaked horribly and I almost fell off the chair, my heart beating loudly in my chest.

"Damn," I whispered, gripping the shotgun tight in case somebody had heard.

I waited. One minute, two, five. I pushed the shotgun in front of me and used my hands to pull myself up. A quick push off with the tips of my toes was just enough to get most of my chest on the trash littered pavement.

"I told you, I heard something," a voice said in the darkness.

I wasn't in a panic, but there were at least two people by the sound of it, walking this way. I could just make out the beam of a flashlight from somewhere around the corner of the buildings. I'd noted that I'd come out in an alleyway, and I didn't see anywhere to hide except...

"Yeah, I wasn't sure if that was you hearing things again. You're so paranoid, Larry," another voice answered.

"Shut up you two," a third said, "If Gary finds out we were slacking on our rounds, he'll shoot us. Don't be loud, and don't draw attention. If somebody's out here, we'll find him."

Three figures moved in front of the alleyway and I shut my eyes when the light passed on and over me. I opened them up and looked from underneath the trash bag I'd pulled on top of me. The bag had been mostly dry, but something rank wafted to my nostrils from it.

"Hey, look!"

I could move my eyes to the side enough to see that the flashlight was now lighting up the open window of the building I'd just left.

"Was that open before?" Larry asked.

"The fuck should I know?" the third figure replied, "Jay, you remember this place?"

"Yeah," Jay, the second figure said, "It's the old flophouse where Tanya's family stayed. She was on the upstairs."

"I meant the basement window, you dumb fuck."

"Oh, well, it wouldn't surprise me. They had bums and needle freaks getting in all the time."

"One of us should go call this in," Larry said.

"You volunteering? You going to wake the boss up? How do we even know somebody is nearby?"

"I told you, I heard something."

"Then you can go wake the boss up, get the whole damned gang awake... and when we go into the basement and nobody's there, it's on your ass."

"I'm not the one who fell the fuck asleep when I was supposed to be doing my rounds."

An arm lashed out in the semi-darkness and the flashlight fell as Larry was decked in the face. The strike sounded like a slap, but I could hear the surprised breath that left him as the pain kicked in.

"Motherfucker," he snarled.

Noise discipline was gone and I was about to bury myself further when the second man rushed in to break it up. He tripped over my legs, unburying me. He fell with a scream and the third figure turned to yell or lash out at him. When he turned on his flashlight, I was already moving. I didn't want to use the shotgun if I had to, but I had a feeling I was going to have to, and soon.

Instead of running, I rolled once while pulling my knife. As the man who'd knocked down the first started pulling his pistol to bear on me, I sunk the blade into his thigh and twisted. His face screwed up in a rictus of pain and instead of screaming, a hiss of air left him as he tried not to cry out. He was already falling, and I pulled him towards me as I rose to my feet, one hand reaching for the wrist that held the gun.

He tried to pull the trigger, but I now had my feet under me. My knife flashed out and sank into his chest to the hilt. I pulled the pistol free and turned. The man who'd tripped over me was patting the ground around him, looking for something he dropped. The man who'd been punched was quickly getting to his feet and a handgun materialized out of the darkness behind his back and he held it out on me.

"Who the fuck are you?" he asked, his voice cold. At his feet, the other man started making whimpering noises

"Just some bum who was looking for food or a fix," I said in a hopeful voice, my palms sweaty.

"Yeah, right. Hey... Carl?" The gun wavered for half a second as he shot a glance back to the man who was crawling on his hands and knees.

"Almost found it," the man said, and then made a triumphant sound as he rose, holding an old chromed Saturday night special on me.

"So, who the fuck are you really?" the man asked, taking half a step closer so his gun was within swatting range.

True tip, don't get within swatting range with a pistol. Only idiots would do that in an attempt to intimidate somebody. Since I wasn't afraid to die, I wasn't intimidated.

"I was homeless before the EMP. I'm just looking for food, a fix, someplace to stay. The last place I was at had a ton of rats, but man... I didn't know this was the marked territory."

"Drop the gun. You killed him, and you're going to regret that," he said.

"He was an ass," the second man said, his gun pointing towards me. "How did you get so close?"

This was not going well.

"I came in two or three days ago. I've been camped out in the basement," I lied.

In the darkness and confined spaces, I might have a better chance.

"Drop the gun, asshole." I felt the cheap pistol press into the back of my head.

I dropped it, letting it clatter onto the pavement. I held my arm up as the man grabbed the sling of my shotgun and removed it. I was going to fucking kill these punks. He patted me down and found my backup knife... not the one that was buried in the man. I made sure to keep that in mind as an available asset if I was feeling stabby again soon.

"You've been down there for two or three days?" The man in front of me, Larry, asked.

"Yeah, there's a few cases of food. It's not bad if you don't hate spam and corned beef hash... it would be great if I had eggs to go with it, but I..." I started blathering fast, hopefully sounding nervous and scared.

"Is there anybody else down there?" The man behind me asked, resting a hand on my left shoulder, and grinding the pistol into the back of my skull.

"No," I told them truthfully.

"Let's go," the man behind me said, pushing my shoulder.

I started to kneel down by the window but was kicked in the face. The man behind me lost his grip as I fell backward. I could taste the blood sheeting down across my lips and in the back of my throat from the broken nose. The pain was bad, but it was something I could compartmentalize and keep at bay. It was the watery eyes I had to worry about. It limited my vision and I got to my feet slowly, with my hands up.

"Ok, then you show me where to go," I told them.

They led me around to the front of the building, and into the public hallway. A staircase went up on the left-hand side and the lower level was mostly open space with a door and a sign on that read 'Manager.' Another sign read 'Basement Storage.'

"Down there," the second man told me, pushing me again.

I opened the door, wishing I had my pen light out, and took to the stairs slowly. I weighed my options and decided the stairs might be the perfect place to make my move, but I hadn't expected them to make me go first. That threw things off a bit. Not by much, though. I wished I'd paid better attention to what was on or in front of the stairs.

"Can I get some light, it's kinda hard to see, man," I said trying my best to sound like 'the Dude' from *The Big Lebowski*.

"Shut up," Larry hissed from behind me.

"One of us should go get Gary and the guys. We're breaking protocol. Especially with him stabbing Carl," Jay, the second man, said.

"Yeah, hurry back, get reinforcements, man," I said, grinning to myself.

If I was about to die, I might as well enjoy it. If on the other hand, Jay or Larry were stupid enough to leave me alone with just one of them, I would make my play.

"Shut up," Larry said, a gun pressed into the back of my head.

"Hey man, be cool. What you looking for?" I asked.

"Make sure you're all alone, your stash of food," Jay said quietly.

"You ain't cannibals, are ya?" I asked, trying to make myself sound scared.

"Shut up, just show us where you sleep." The gun was back grinding into my hair just above where I had it tied off in a ponytail.

"Over there," I pointed.

I'd reached the bottom of the stairs and I waited for them to follow me down. Jay, by the sound of it, was still at the last step, but I could feel Larry's gun on the back of my head still.

"Go check it out," Larry said from behind me.

I was jostled to the side as Jay pushed by, and the gun left my head for a second. I put my hands up and turned my head to look back at Larry.

"You're really going to rob a homeless dude?" I asked him.

"You can't rob the dead," Larry said with a wicked grin and cocked the gun, "You can loot their corpse, though."

I turned half my body with my hands up so I could somewhat face him. I considered going for the gun, but Jay yelled.

"The fuck is this?" he asked, pointing down.

"The sub-basement," I told him, without turning my gaze from Larry.

"What's down there?" he asked.

"Rats, my sleeping bag, the food."

"There's no fucking way I'm going down that hole, man," Jay said, turning to us.

I could see him out of the corner of my eye. He'd started moving back toward us, pistol in one hand, flashlight in the other when a shadow disengaged from the darkness and swarmed up behind him. An arm clad in black wrapped around his neck and he let out a shrill scream before it abruptly cut off. The gun at my face wavered and I lashed out with my hands.

The gun went off twice as I pushed it in the air and when Larry tried to bring the gun down, I locked my grip on his gun hand and fell backward, lifting my knees to catch his weight and kept the momentum going. Momentum is a funny thing. It allows you to move objects that you may not be able to lift, or to move objects much further and faster than you could with just your own muscle power. Thankfully, I managed a little of both.

Garbage and boxes crunched under my weight, but as my back hit with Larry almost on top, I pushed up with my legs and arched my back, twisting and pulling. When I came up, I'd pulled the gun under the man's chin and held it there. I wasn't sure what had happened to Jay exactly, but I chanced a glance to see the flashlight being picked up by a figure dressed in black, with a knit ski mask over his or her features. The shotgun was loosely held in the figure's hands.

"You come any closer, I blow him away," I said,

the gunshots still ringing in my ears.

"Don't kill me, man," Larry said from below me, his voice strange because it had a rounded piece of barrel shoved into the tender hollow spot under his chin at the base of his neck.

"Dick," the figure said in a familiar raspy voice and Jeremy pulled the mask off to expose his features.

"That's it, you're grounded," I said in relief.

"I'm a grown ass man," Jeremy said and spat on the floor.

He knelt down and pulled a black blade out of Jay's back, wiped it on the corpse's shirt and sheathed it.

"Come on man, you kill me, this place is going to be swarming. They probably already heard the shots. You let me go, I'll tell them you ran off. They don't need to know that—"

I slugged him with my free hand viciously, turning his face sideways with the force.

"He's right," Jeremy rasped, looking out one of the side windows. "People are coming."

"Well, there's only one thing we can do," I told him.

"Shoot him?" Jeremy asked me, an eyebrow raised.

"Naw, we're just gonna put him down," I said, smiling.

"Put me down? Come on man, I don't..."

The flashlight was pointed at him and I could see my punch had gashed his mouth. He'd probably cut himself with his own teeth. They were stained a reddish pink.

"If you make one more sound, I'm going to pig stick you like I did your friend out there," I told him viciously.

CHAPTER 12

"Come on, Larry. Wake up," I said, slapping the man lightly.

He startled awake. We'd tied his arms and legs to a lightweight armchair and left him in the darkness when he had started blubbering about rats. I guessed it was a phobia for him. I'd sent Jeremy off, but Danielle and I sat alone in the dark.

"What are you doing, man? Who is it?" he asked.

We hadn't bothered putting a light on for him. I decided living in the dark gave you better night vision than you'd expect. For example, I could kind of make out his features in the gloom. We were in an old storm sewer and a little sunlight was filtering down through a manhole cover over a hundred yards behind him. It was enough for us.

"It's still just me. The guy you were trying to rob and kill."

"What the fuck you want?" he snarled.

"I want you to answer some questions for me," I told him quietly.

"And then you'll let me go?" he asked.

"Probably not. But if you want to do this the hard way, I'll let her take care of you."

"Her?" he asked and Danielle snapped on an electric LED lantern I'd kept in case of emergencies because the scarcity of batteries.

"You recognize me?" Danielle asked.

The man flinched, but there was no recognition in it. It was probably the fact that she was holding Jeremy's knife up close to his face that did it.

"I… No, not really," he said, and I could hear the truth of it.

"Do you kidnap, torture, and rape women and children?" I asked him.

"No, no… I swear."

"Really? So your gang at the museum haven't been hit by an old vet a handful of times?"

"You! But last I saw you…" A horror-stricken expression hit his face as I made sure my features were well-lit.

He'd just admitted that he was a part of that gang and also, that he knew of me. He'd also figured out, that in those six words, he'd just sealed his fate.

"Yeah, a shave does wonders, doesn't it? Listen, the kid has some questions for you. If you don't answer, she'll use the knife."

"What happens if I do tell you?" he asked hopefully.

I pulled a .45 from my belt and showed it to him.

"It'll be quick and painless. She was held for a time by guys like you. You don't want to know what she'll do."

The man's eyes were almost rolling into the back of his head in fear. I couldn't blame him, but he needed to talk.

"I can't… I mean, they'll kill me," he whispered.

I shrugged. "You're dead either way. I'm giving you the chance to make it quick and painless. Otherwise, I'll let the girl get involved."

"You, I mean… No. If I'm dead anyway, no. I won't talk."

"He's all yours," I said to Danielle and walked away into the darkness.

* * *

I was waiting around a bend in the tunnel when the pleas stopped and the sharp report of gunfire startled me so bad I almost fell. It was loud in the confines of the tunnel and I pulled my .45 and started running, with only forty short feet to cover. Only forty feet. My body knew what to do though my mind was racing. Larry didn't have a gun, I'd checked him myself – unless I *thought* I'd checked him and he'd squirreled one away and I hadn't found it.

"Danielle," I whimpered as I rounded the corner.

I already had the .45 raised and was ready to fire, but I hit the safety back on as soon as I saw Danielle standing over Larry's slumped form.

"Danielle," I said, noticing the gun in her hand, it was one of the revolvers I'd brought back. "What…?"

"He gave them up," she said.

"But… You were just going to scare him. You weren't going to—"

"It was my choice, Dick," she said, wiping her eyes. "In the end, he begged for it to be me who'd do it."

That stopped me short. "Why?" I asked finally.

"He said that with all the evil he's done," she said and her chest hitched and I could see her fighting back her tears, "He said it would be fitting for me to do it. It was Karma, and…"

She held the gun out to me. I took it and pulled her close in a hug. I wanted to ask her if he had given up the answers, but I knew he probably had if she'd ended him. I heard footsteps far off behind us, but I held her as she cried into my chest. Something inside of me was threatening to break, a dam about to burst. I held it back somehow.

I knew Jeremy was back there somewhere, but he was expecting me to do the shooting. Hopefully, I could get her out of here with him, so I could clean up. As it was, she'd hit him perfectly. One shot to the heart, and she'd been so close that there were powder burns on his shirt.

"I'm sorry, you shouldn't have had to do that," I whispered.

"No, I did. That was one thing that he was right about. He might not have been one of the men who… who hurt me… but… I'm not that girl anymore."

"No, no you're not," I said taking her weight as her legs wobbled.

Before she fainted, I'd already started bending at the knees to catch her. Sudden adrenaline or even shock can cause it.

"Oh God, I'm sorry," she said a moment later, wiping her nose with her shirt sleeve and pulling on my arms to get her feet back under her.

She was still crying, but it wasn't the deep wrenching sobs like it had been a minute before. She put her arms around me and cried some more. I looked at Larry. If you looked at him from the shoulders up, he almost looked like he was sleeping peacefully.

"You're ok," I murmured and rubbed my hands over the top of her head, smoothing her hair back before she got snot and tears in it.

"He talked. I wrote a lot of stuff down," she said. "I didn't have to hurt him with the knife."

I had noticed that, other than the marks of the scuffle and being bound, he was still in pretty good shape.

"Let's go back and talk. I think Jeremy's coming."

"Oh God," she said, wiping her eyes and rubbing her face.

"Do you have any water?" she asked.

I smiled and handed her the bottle I kept in

my pack. She poured some on her hands and then rubbed her face before throwing her head back, whipping her hair over her shoulder.

"Better," she said.

"If you're sure," I told her. "But if you ever want to talk… I know what it's like."

"The bad dreams?" she asked me.

"Those are mostly… guilt dreams. Why did I live, why did so and so die…? Could I have fixed or changed anything? I guess the usual stuff," I admitted.

"Guilt? You were fighting a war," she whispered, hugging me then breaking all contact.

"Yeah, and you were fighting one, too. Winning doesn't stop the dreams, though. Killing changes someone. I'm just so sorry you had to do this."

She looked over her shoulder at Larry, then back at me. "I don't think I'll have any problems sleeping. It is horrible, but with one less guy like him in the world, it seems like it might be a little easier to sleep at night."

"I think it's too early to know that," I said. "But yeah, I know it'll make me sleep easier."

Danielle looked up at me, the edges of her lips tugging up in what could only have been a half of a smile.

* * *

We'd had to rehydrate some of the jerky strips to add to the soup. The traps had been empty for a couple of days, and instead of going out to new locations to set my snares, I'd been watching the museum. Danielle had done her job, but the man had either lied and done it well enough to fool her, or he hadn't known shit. Larry had only gone to a few drop offs with the slaves and his point of contact had been a guy named Manny. I assumed he was Latino, but I also knew where assumptions could get one in life. He'd also given us the basics of their gang and I was a little blown away.

When most people think of gangs, they think of black youths, hard cases... or Latinos... This was a gang of redneck trailer trash at its core, but one with a progressive recruiting policy. They actually didn't care about skin color so much, especially since the EMP had taken out the grid and all rule of law. They would recruit anyone who could bring value to the gang. First, though, they had to go through an initiation phase. Kind of how bikers have to earn their patches. I'd never have thought it'd take the end of the world as we know it to dilute the effects of racism, but it had.

To earn a spot, each new prospect had to bring in a woman or child or give the location on where some were hiding for the main gang to pick up. A lot of times, the scum had turned on their own families and then just skipped the after party and breaking them in. The really sick ones didn't skip. It made my planning easier to know that I'd be killing pure evil. Still, the gang's strengths were also its weakness. They had a lot of members left.

Before the event, there had probably been ten to twenty core members, with hanger-on's and girlfriends that numbered upwards of a hundred souls all told – if they still had their souls. Hunger had gotten to a lot of them and they were down to thirty or forty, with their various sidekicks included. Still, horribly huge numbers for one man to consider.

But I had quite a few things in the plus side column if I was to keep a tally. None of them were military, or law enforcement, or had any formal training.

Most of them were only lightly armed with handguns or knives. One dude even walked around with a Katana like he thought he was in *The Walking Dead*. The few rifles they had were scoped and quite a few of the guys were deadly accurate with them, but none of them had been under accurate return fire or had been fired on first.

Now for the cons. There were thirty to forty of them. Most of them were armed. They were evil and wouldn't hesitate to bury someone or turn on their own family, if it meant they could get another meal, another fix, another bottle of booze.

Which brought me to the slave issue. Currently, in the old cafeteria, they were holding ten to fifteen women and young ladies. Apparently, when they took the odd male, he was always under eighteen and was kept separate from the ladies. All were held until the gang got word from Manny, and then they were shipped up to the docks where an exchange of goods was made. Two truckloads of humanity for two truckloads of food and supplies, ammunition and medication.

That in of itself just blew my mind. I understood

how the black market worked… I was a junkie for a long time. You get the stuff from your dealer. The dealer uses your money to buy more stuff. But somewhere in this situation, Manny's people had become the dealer's dealer and I was wondering how the hell they had the materials and manpower for all of that. On top of it, if they had two or three gangs supplying them somewhat regularly, where were the slaves going?

One last piece of good news was that the former punks had wiped out a third gang right after I'd hit Curtis's group. At first, they'd thought it had been them consolidating and taking more territory. Knowing that they were slightly larger and better armed, they'd staged things and hit the other gang when they were having a party. Sound familiar? They killed or absorbed everyone from that gang and took all of their supplies and slaves. That's why they had so many currently waiting on word from Manny.

I was torn. Did I let the fifteen souls go to Manny, so I could find the source? Should I stop them like I did with Jamie and Mel? Should I go in before any word came entirely? None of them and all of them were both the right and wrong decision for a list of reasons too numerous for me to count. For the third day in a row since we'd snatched Larry and killed his two buddies, I was watching the museum. I'd changed rooftops and vantage points until I could see more.

I was almost too far away to shoot, but when I saw a car I didn't recognize pull up, I tensed, waiting. I'd heard it coming, but I'd missed where it came from. One man walked in, getting the nod from the four guards at the east entrance. I debated going down to get closer to ground level, but I'd seen that car come in and now I could pay close attention to where it went, unless—

The man walked out again smiling and got in the car. Three stories. That's all I had to get down in a hurry if I wanted to chase him on the ground. Three stories of pounding on the metal fire escape, drawing all kinds of attention. Nobody was paying attention to my direction now, but if I made a racket I'd be dead. Instead, I watched. It looked like a late model BMW, probably a diesel judging by the black smoke that puffed with every gear shift. Its silver color would make it easy enough to find if it was kept in the open, which it might not be.

"Is that Manny?" Jeremy asked me.

"I think so," I told him.

"Flashy wheels he has," he said, a little pissy sounding.

"Probably old enough not to have a computer and diesel fuel lasts for a long time. Smart," I said in admiration. "Smart too, that it's so pretty. Makes our job easier."

"Danielle should be able to see further," he told me.

I looked at him, wondering if he was being serious.

"Don't worry, Jamie is with the kids. Danielle's on a rooftop like us. She went half a mile further and is in a corner office. That brown building there, eight windows up," he said in a whisper.

I rolled to my side a bit, careful not to roll on the gun, and peeked. A flash of light shone from within the building, the glass having been knocked out by explosions, fires, or looters. I gave a half-hearted wave and looked back at the museum in front of us.

"When did you two set this up?" I asked him, pissed that they didn't follow orders. Again.

"I didn't. She told me about the idea. It wasn't until a second ago that I realized she was up there. She told me she was thinking of using her makeup mirror like a signal mirror. We've been talking…"

"Yeah?" I asked, somewhat impressed.

"Well, before radios, it was all hand signals, signal mirrors, and smoke signs," he said sheepishly.

"So, you told her a little military history from your ROTC days, and she took it from there?"

"Well, I hope that's her, and not one of those rednecks with a scoped rifle," he said, trying to make a joke of it, but it hit me hard.

"Oh shit," I said. A cold trickle of fear had gotten to me.

He'd said it was her, so I'd never considered that. Then he'd told me she was there because it was what he'd expected her to do, based off a conversation… Should we flee? Wait it out? I cursed myself for having gone so soft. I couldn't afford mistakes like this, not now, not ever.

I turned my binoculars and tried to glass the building I'd seen the flash in.

"How do you know it's her?" I asked him quietly.

"She mentioned that office building specifically," Jeremy said, smiling.

I rolled onto my back, so I could look to the building and to Jeremy without having to move much. I knew I was exposing myself a little to the roll, but no shots were fired.

"If I were running the gang, I'd have all the high buildings near my hideout occupied with lookouts and snipers. Did you or Danielle check it out ahead of time? I mean, what if their leader is at least as smart as a homeless bum who eats whatever is stupid enough to go into his traps and nets?"

I watched the color drain out of Jeremy's face and I knew what he was feeling. It was the same thing as me. Horror, worry, fear. On top of all of that, we'd just gotten our first look at Manny. If that signal was from a mirror, it could have been seen by the nearly half a dozen men near the outside entrance.

"We have to get down there," I said, "If I saw that mirror, they could have, too."

"Not from this angle. Besides, we'd hear gunfire if somebody came near her. She has that .45 again."

I wanted to curse aloud. What did that impulsive fucking kid think she was doing? I knew she'd wanted to help… but truth be told, both of them had been acting rather irrationally lately…

Then it hit me. I'd been working towards moving on. It was why I was finally taking the plunge to go after the slaves. And I'd been holding them back because they were staying. It was as simple as that and selfish in nature. I felt disgusted with myself.

If something happened to them, I couldn't go find Maggie and Mary.

"Did she say when she was going to meet up with us?" I asked him.

"No. Like I said, I never even knew she was going to do it till I saw the flash when that silver car was driving down the road. You were watching through the binoculars. Did anyone react then?"

"No, all eyes were on the car," I said.

"See? We should be safe."

"How did she know what building we were going to be on top of?" I asked him. "We change positions."

"I told her I thought we'd be coming to this one. It's got a good angle on the museum, it's high enough up here on the roof to be out of the normal sight range unless you're far off, and if you're far off you're not likely to see it. Fire escape… the works. I noticed it last time we were out patrolling."

Which meant I was becoming predictable. Shit… then I reconsidered. The kid was ROTC during his high school years and he'd walked the same terrain I had. I'd been inadvertently grooming him for when I left. Maybe, it was that weird sort of telepathy or synchronized thinking that the tabloid shows had talked about. Instead of wrestling or chest thumping, we'd picked out places to plan mayhem and mass murder for bonding time. Go me.

"Let's see if we can get her attention and meet up somewhere. I want to go looking for that car and the other gang before we take these guys out."

"Take them out? How are you going to do that? We're totally outnumbered."

"I know, but finding that car is the first thing we have to do, and then we need to find out where everyone is."

"So you good? With Danielle being up there? You're not going to yell at her, are you?"

"Maggie's always been a headstrong girl, it's about damned time I gave her some credit," I said, rolling over and getting to my knees and then crawling back towards the fire escape. "Otherwise, it'll drive me crazy with worry every time she's out of my sight."

It would too. My daughter could be snarky and headstrong, but Mary had raised her right without me being around for much of it. I had to give my ex all the credit there. I just wished I'd had the—

"You mean Danielle, right?" Jeremy interrupted.

"I… yeah. Slip of the tongue. I've been thinking about my daughter a lot lately," I lied.

CHAPTER 13

I'm sorry Dick, I just don't see it as that big of a deal," Danielle fumed.

We'd met her at the base of the office complex. She'd come out of hiding when Jeremy and I walked out into the open with our rifles at the easy ready position.

"Did you clear the building first? Like we did with that apartment building last week?" I demanded.

"I cleared everything up to where I was hiding out, Dick. The building's been looted and gutted."

I looked at her hard, wondering if she was pulling one over on me.

"There's nothing up there but places for the pigeons to roost and shit all over," she said.

"Pigeons?" I asked her, storing that away for

later if we wanted to add some squab to our menus.

"Yeah, why?"

"I'll tell you later," I said. "Did you see where that car went?" I asked her for the second time.

"Yeah, but I lost it when it turned. I can show you. I don't have the streets memorized."

"Can you show it to me in the dark?" I asked. "We've been out here a while, and I don't want to tempt fate by moving in the daylight too much."

"Is there a storm drain or sewer that runs that way for half a mile?" Jeremy asked.

"Not anything I know how to get into," I told him. "It wasn't part of the CTA system. Maybe if I were a city engineer I might know, but..."

"Shhhh," Danielle said, motioning all of us forward.

I gave half a glance behind me before following her inside the old office building. Jeremy and I followed her in through the rubble-strewn lobby and bypassed the elevators. They were out anyways, but I wasn't looking forward to eight flights of steps.

"Hurry, they're coming," she said.

"Who?" Jeremy asked.

I went up the damned steps with her, glass crunching softly under my boots.

"Search party, I think."

If she was right, it was just some of them sweeping through the area. Often times, looting what was left behind and being opportunistic thugs when they could be. Jeremy got it and hurried. She didn't lead us to her last spot like I was expecting, but to a corner office on the third floor. The shades flapped uselessly and noisily in the broken out window frames. Chicago came by its nickname, 'the windy city' honestly.

"Over here," Danielle said, motioning.

Two desks, rather large desks, had been shoved against the wall with a ton of stuff heaped on top of them. There was a hollowed out spot where the feet would go and it was into there that she scampered. I knelt down and followed her in. With the two desks pushed together, I expected the space to be tight, but it wasn't horrible. That coming from a guy who lives underground.

"Why here?" I asked her.

"I know this place," she said and then pulled over some scraps of paper and pushed them along the bottom edge, making a garbage barrier. We were all shoulder to shoulder, trying to turn around to face the front.

"You think somebody's been in here?" I heard a voice ask.

"No, but it doesn't hurt to look," another said.

"Man, I don't see shit. You wanna go up to the top and get some birds?" a voice asked, one that sounded hokey enough to have come right out of a bad comedy act.

"You and your hunting," a different voice said. "If you want to go up eight flights of stairs for a few birds that don't have much meat on them, go ahead. Rico's still got a ton of food for us."

I heard the footsteps pass the doorway to where we were hiding.

"Want to slip out while they walk around?" Jeremy whispered to me softly.

"No, we wait," I whispered back. Both of them nodded.

I could hear the echoes on their footfalls from the stairwell and then above us. Something crashed loudly below and they all busted up laughing. It made me tense up and reach for the strap of the sling. I could get the shotgun to me in a hurry, but the report inside of the small desk cave would be deafening.

Soon, the footfalls were coming back our way and the men were laughing, talking about how much they'd scared the shit out of Ronnie. I was assuming they'd chucked something out of the fourth-floor window at someone and were laughing their asses off about it. All we had to do was stay frosty… and my mind slipped.

* * *

I was laying on the floor of the bank, waiting for the mortar teams to take out the sniper's nest. Both my battle buddies were down hard and Mike was still moving his legs weakly. The gunfire from the three men inside, combined with ours in the small confines had been deafening, and I could see his lips moving, but I couldn't make out his words. I crawled over to him, my M4 in my right hand. His lips moved again and he pulled at a pouch on his vest. I pressed my left hand over the hole in his stomach to staunch the flow of blood, but there was so much of it.

"I can't hear you, man," I told him.

He still kept reaching for the pouch, so I dropped my carbine and pulled it open for him. There was only one thing inside. It was a picture of a beautiful red-headed woman and his young kid. From the hat, I couldn't tell if it was a boy or girl, but it's what he wanted, so I gave it to him. He held it up, the blood on his hands marking the bottom of the picture. He held it up to his eyes and mumbled again. I could barely make out his words, but the ringing in my ears was starting to recede and I could make out consonants. Something moved in my peripheral vision and I stood up.

One of the three men who'd played jack in the box with us wasn't dead yet. He was thrashing on the ground, trying to pull his AK-47 close to him with a booted foot. That motion and what little of my hearing was left, was what had made me turn and look. I grabbed my M4 and walked over towards him, kicking the gun out of his way.

He looked up at me in shock. His two friends were down hard and he was badly wounded. He had three rounds stitched into his chest from a burst. I made sure he didn't die painfully and when I was done, I wiped my knife off on his shirt and sheathed it.

"Mike, come on, man," I said noticing him staring at me. "Don't give up, I radioed it in."

I didn't see the rising and falling of his chest. I walked over, his eyes never wavering as I moved. I knelt down, one hand scarlet from trying to stop the bleeding on him, the other splattered where I'd made someone else bleed profusely.

"Mike?" I asked, feeling for a pulse.

He was gone. Just like that. I'd turned my head, took the pressure off the wound to kill the last man… and he was gone. In his right hand, he still held the picture. I pulled it from him with the cleanest fingers I had and put it in an empty mag pouch of mine, trying to be careful not to fold it.

"I'll let them know for you," I told him, shutting his eyes with two red smears.

I went to my other bud. He'd taken the rounds in the head and had been gone instantly. He had been a loner, joining the military to get the GI bill. He loved it so much he'd never left. He'd denied promotions, done everything I had or was wanting to do. Be a good soldier, get in the middle of the shit. Make a difference, one ugly, bloody battle at a time.

"Six, you have sniper's position in sight?" I heard through the earwig that had been silent for a while.

"Affirmative. Call in the adjustments as you see them."

"go go go go go go go go go go"….

* * *

"Come on, Dick," Jeremy was whispering into my ear, rocking my body hard with his hand. "We have to go. You're freaking out Danielle."

"She's…" I looked around.

We were alone inside in the hollowed out space. Otherwise, he wouldn't have had room to do that.

"Are they gone?" I asked him.

"Yeah, a couple minutes ago. You just sorta… went to sleep or something," Jeremy's voice was scared sounding.

"Sorry, got lost in my thoughts. Danielle?" I whispered louder for her.

"Here."

"Wait for me, they might have left someone behind to intercept anyone coming out of hiding."

"Oh shit, yeah, I'm waiting." she whispered.

Getting out was harder than getting in and I made a little noise when my gun banged against the desks. Finally, I got out and stretched. The popping of my joints was almost as loud as when Jeremy went to stand and stumbled into Danielle, knocking them both to the ground. They ended up in a heap with Jeremy landing on his soft head. I smiled as a goofy grin filled Jeremy's features when Danielle got off of him.

"Shhhh, dumbass," Danielle said, brushing her pants off.

"You both be quiet," I said, moving past them, towards the window.

I looked out, and seven men were crossing the street ahead of us, most of them with pistols or knives tucked into their waistbands or holstered on their belts/sheaths. None of them looked as gnarled as the group I'd taken down already. These guys were moderately well groomed, which was the first thing I noticed. Five of them sported beards, but close-cropped. I pulled out my binoculars and was able to confirm that at least two of them had been recently clean shaven as well.

Their hair was also cut neatly, a detail I tucked away in the back of my mind. None of their clothing stood out, but they walked with a confidence that was evident in their swagger. Nobody had messed with them and other than taking out that one gang, they weren't expecting anything big to go down. I hadn't really put two and two together until now, but the rest of the gang was groomed somewhat normal as well. Something to think of. Maybe they had a barber or cosmologist in there…

"Do we wait here?" Danielle asked from behind me.

"No, I think there's something I gotta do first," I told her.

"What's that?"

"Did Larry ever tell you his last name?" I asked her, changing the subject.

"Uh… Michaels, I think," she told me with a puzzled look on her face. "What do you have to do?"

"I need to go find Jamie," I told her. "My hair's a bit too long."

"I think he's lost it," I heard Jeremy whisper. I wasn't supposed to hear it, so I ignored it.

* * *

"You know, without clippers, I can't get it too close," Jamie said.

She'd taken no time to cut the longest parts of my hair off and had begun trimming it down. I'd asked her for a finger length on the sides and back and two or three inches up top to style or spike. She'd nodded and had been going without comment until now.

"That's fine. Just get the sides as close as you can and blend it in." I told her.

"Sir, yes sir!" she said, but she wasn't joking, she was pissed.

"I'm sorry if I'm being too much of a pain…"

"You've got everybody freaked out," Mel told me, pulling a bucket up close and sat on it in front of me.

"Why's that?" I asked.

"You won't tell Jeremy and Danielle what you're planning, and now you're getting all spiffed up like you have a hot date."

"I do have a hot date," I told her.

"See, that's just weird. You're scaring us."

"The little kids aren't scared," I said, pointing.

"They're playing board games. Oh, by the way, Salina was down here today. She made it all the way down. Mom heard her calling out and got her back here."

I winced. I'd forgotten about meeting with her, but I'd been obsessed with taking the scum out.

"Mouse seems to be in a good mood. Did it go well?" I asked the mother-daughter pair.

They hesitated in answering me and finally it was Jamie who replied, her hands massaging my scalp as she made cuts with a sharp pair of scissors.

"Yes. She brought her son, too. You should have seen Pauly's eyes light up. I think he likes the idea of a big brother for a protector."

"How did Mouse act around him?" I asked.

"Very scared at first, but he just sat down at the edge of the mezzanine away from everyone else. Salina couldn't get him to come and meet them. I think he kind of understood that he was scaring her."

"So how did she…?"

"Pauly stole her hairbrush and gave it to Jerome," Mel said with a smile touching the corner of her lips.

"That'll do it," I said smiling.

"But, Dick," Mel said standing and pushing the bucket out of the way. "Why won't you tell them what the plan is? I mean, Jeremy said it was like you had a seizure when you all were hiding out. They're all just worried that…"

"I'll snap and hurt you guys?" I asked her suddenly.

Jamie stopped cutting and I could feel her moving back as her hands left me.

"No, I don't think that's what they're worried about," Jamie said, walking in front so she could see me.

"No? Then why isn't my word good enough? I have a plan, and every time I try to go through with one, I get party crashers. This one, I can't have any extras. I won't have room and I'm going to be moving too hard and too fast."

"So there is a conscious reason," Jamie said, pulling a black plastic comb out of her back pocket.

"Yes, it's not just me doing something off the

wall," I told her. "There is a plan in place."

"Is it more of you running and gunning?" Mel asked.

I looked her over. She'd recently washed and was in a new change of clothes. Removing the layers of grime had done a lot for the young lady. If anything, she looked even younger than fifteen. Despite that, I could see the intelligence shining brightly behind her hazel eyes. It was like she was a human lie detector and she was judging on whether or not I was being truthful.

"Some of it," I said ruefully as Jamie stood right in front of me and worked on my bangs.

I closed my eyes, so I wouldn't stare and let her finish the haircut.

"How's that look?" Danielle asked me, holding up a mirror.

I hadn't known she was behind me, but it made sense. It wasn't a huge space and I was undergoing my extreme makeover.

"I look like... Not me," I told her, surprised.

Staring back at me in her makeup mirror was an image of me that I hadn't seen in well over twenty years. I had enough sandy brown hair to style and my beard was close-cropped. Crow's feet were pulling at the edges of my eyes and laugh lines had formed near the edges of my mouth, only to be mostly covered with a ginger-colored facial hair.

"Ooooohhhh, is that Uncle Dick?" I heard somebody say and then the slapping of footsteps.

Jamie backed up, scissors and comb in her hands held high as Mouse launched herself.

"Stop, you'll get hair all over—"

The wind was almost knocked out of me as she landed in my lap heavily. My arms went out automatically to catch her from bouncing or falling off. Trust. Total unwavering trust. She knew I'd always catch her, even if it hurt. I hugged her tight.

"Uncle Dick, you're squishing my guts out," she said.

I let her go and looked at her. Her café au lait colored skin was glowing and her eyes no longer looked bloodshot. Her fever had broken a couple days ago, and other than digestive issues from the diet and antibiotics, she was definitely healthier than she'd been a week ago.

"Maybe I just want to squish you one more time," I told her, giving her one more hug till she pretended to gag, and then I let her go.

"So, you don't want us crashing your party?" Jeremy asked as I put Mouse down on the floor.

"No, not at all. I'm going to be stirring up a hornet's nest. Worst case scenario, I'll have a hundred bad guys hunting me. I can't do what I want to do if I'm worrying about you guys," I told him truthfully.

"What about the car?" Danielle asked. "Don't you need to know where it was?" Her voice was quiet.

"I do, but I don't know if I'll need to do that tonight. Here, let me show you what I was thinking," I said standing and brushing the hair off of me.

I walked over to my spot, the hammock near the mez. I kept my big pack near there. In the front, in a large Ziploc bag, I kept my maps. I pulled out one of them and walked back over to the mez where everyone was waiting. The little kids paid us no mind. They were having battleship battles, rolling dice matching numbers and reading. Their quiet buzz almost drowned out the silence that settled in down here. Almost.

"Here's the museum," I said, pointing after I'd spread out the map.

"Yup," Jeremy said.

"Here's where you and I were at," I pointed and they nodded. "You were in this building… so they drove towards the docks, yes?" I asked.

"Yeah…" Danielle said, her words trailing off as the confusion she was feeling became evident.

"Well, if they turned here, there's only one or two places I think they could be going."

"Wait, you're going to that warehouse," Jeremy said. "I drove by there once as a kid, it's an industrial section of town. It's a big open…"

"No, I'm not going there," I lied. "I'm going to check it out as a potential. There's also a meat processing plant. Big refrigerated sections, and here," I said, pointing to another building to the north, "is one of the buildings next to the wharf. All could be potential areas where the big group is working out of."

"Do they have a name?" Jamie asked. "You just say gang, group, shitheads, or assholes when you talk about them."

Mel snickered and we all shared a grin.

"They call themselves the 'Consortium,'" Danielle said, still grinning.

"Sounds scary," Mel said.

"I don't know. It doesn't sound like a gang to me."

"It sounds more like a business than anything else to me," I told her.

"That's what that Larry guy was talking about, he said they were..." Her words trailed off as she was trying to find the right word, "almost like a Russian mob or something like that. It was really weird."

"Like the Russian mob?" I asked her smiling.

"That'll make life interesting," Jeremy said. "Are you sure that you don't want help?"

"No, I got this. I don't even know what the consortium looks like, where they operate exactly, or what all I'm going to be getting myself into tonight. If I get a chance to mess with them, I might, but I don't know. I just have a pretty good idea of what I want to do, where I need to go and how I'm going to accomplish it, and I can give you guys all the details. If you really want to help, can someone move the truck, so I can use it for a getaway?"

"Unless either of these kids knows how to drive a stick," Jamie said, "then I'll do it if that's what you really need."

"Yeah, let me show you on the map where I want you to put it and take Jeremy with you. Wear some kind of bulky clothing, nothing loose or tight..." I told her.

CHAPTER 14

I told them to hold off an hour before they moved the truck. I'd been moving slowly on foot through the tunnels until I was near the office building that we'd hidden out in earlier. I'd come up in an alleyway from a manhole cover not too far from there. My biggest concern during the early part of my plan was getting spotted by a roving patrol. Once I was topside, though, things seemed to get a lot easier for me. The sun was setting on the horizon, and the shadows were getting long and dark. In the distance, I could hear shouts coming from the direction of the museum. I didn't even want to think about what was causing that at this point.

Working my way down the dead, empty streets was something I didn't want to do. I felt very exposed topside, but I was loaded for bear tonight. I had my target .22 pistol and my .45 strapped to my side, along with my shotgun on the drop sling. All the extra weight might not even be needed, but I was hoping I could set things up to the point where I'd get to use a lot of it, get rid of some bad guys, get some details on the enemy they could be facing next, and then freeing some hostages.

My plan was simple. Good guys win, bad guys lose an eye. It almost sounded stupid, like it was really too simple. I kinda hoped it would be really simple. For some stupid reason, the men at the museum called themselves 'the uptown boys'. When I'd still been working for the transit authority, I don't even think I'd ever heard of that gang. I knew a lot of things change and changed fast, but that was one thing I'd never paid attention to, even in my old life. I'd gotten the idea from the uptown boys, though…

They had a pickup truck parked out front of the museum that was just about the same color and the same year as the pickup truck from the turds at the bank. It was how the uptown boys had handled the other gang that really gave me the idea of doing what I was about to do. The uptown boys wouldn't mess with the consortium people, which made me think that they were either part of law enforcement, or military, or even private contractors. It sounded too professional, and they'd sounded too well armed.

I didn't want to pick a fight with the consortium directly, but maybe I could use one against the other. That was my plan. All I had to do was find the stupid fucks. That was how I found myself moving shadow to shadow, one spot of cover and concealment to the next. One thing that Danielle had explained to me, right before I'd left, was that hiding closer to the gang was actually safer - if you could keep yourself hidden. All the good and decent people moved away from them as fast as they could, as far as they could. So, the buildings I was passing should be rather empty or at least, not be full of people who would want to poke their noses in my business tonight.

That's why I only hesitated when I took shortcuts through the backs of buildings or in crossing a lobby through broken doors or windows, never moving openly or just walking straight down the middle of the street. That would've been inviting disaster. One of the other things I'd noticed about the uptown boys was that at some point, they'd spent some time clearing the streets around them. From a tactical standpoint that made sense, creating a clear field of vision. A clear field of fire, so you could see people coming and going, as long as you could look straight down the road.

It also made it bad because you could see them coming, and I didn't want to attract attention. There was still too much daylight left, and I had to move slower. It took me close to an hour and a half to make my way down to where the silver BMW had made its turn. I headed down that way towards the abandoned warehouse. I knew I'd lied to Jeremy about it, but I figured he knew I was lying, too. I really did not want him to join me on this trip. I knew that he and Danielle were grown adults, but I hoped they understood that they could get me killed.

Like a lot of things in Chicago, the warehouse was dark, and most of the windows had been broken out. The only thing that stood out to me was the fact that there were lights moving around inside, and I could see a soft glow as if a lantern or a light had been hung near the ground. I was still too far away to make anything out, but I wanted to get a little height in order to see if I could look around and see if that's where the consortium was actually at.

I couldn't make out any vehicles parked around the warehouse, which in itself was suspicious. When the EMP had happened, everything modern and electronic had simply stopped. Sure, people rolled to a stop, but wherever they'd ended up was where their car stayed. Some people had probably tried to push their cars out of the middle of the road, but a lot of folks in Chicago had just left them where they were. Probably thought the government or the city would take care of the mess.

When they'd found out that no one was coming to help, the initial anger reaction had morphed into something more like fear. As if the gunshots and the fires weren't bad enough, then people had started preying on each other. Most people had taken what they wanted out of their stalled vehicles and left them where they were. They'd simply abandoned them. The parking lot of the warehouse was completely empty, and all of the spaces around the outside of the warehouse were empty, too.

It wasn't like the uptown boys' side where the museum was at. The uptown boys had just pushed the cars off to the side of the road and had left them there, leaving the middle of the roadway open. Here, there was nothing. I got my binoculars out and started watching. A flicker of light, very small and not very bright in the growing darkness, alerted me to someone standing outside near one of the roll-up doors. I trained my binoculars over there and was rewarded with the sight of a glowing ember. The ember moved and I realized it was someone smoking a cigarette. It wasn't fully dark yet, but it would be soon.

When full dark finally did come, I decided I would move over there and get a better look for myself. I watched the guy smoking until the ember was thrown, sparks of illumination crushed out under a boot. Then, the figure started walking. I could just barely make out the movement from six blocks away, but if there'd been one of them, there would be more.

What I'd really hoped was that I'd have enough time to do it tonight. I'd never tried to take fifteen people, let alone two gangs, in one shot. I was about to get up and go when I heard a motor in the distance. I tensed, hoping against all hope that it wasn't the uptown boys making their delivery. That was one thing Danielle had never gotten out of Larry. When did they make their deliveries and where did they meet, exactly?

I listened even harder and then I saw the headlights make a turn far off down the road. It wasn't car, it wasn't truck, it was a semi. I couldn't see the make or model, but it had to have been an old one.

"What the hell is this?" I said to no one quietly.

I'd been laying down so I wouldn't profile myself in the window, but I got to my hands and knees to make my way back out of the building I'd been hiding in. If I wanted information, I'd have to get a little bit closer.

* * *

My heart was racing. I had seen the semi-truck pull to a stop in front of the old warehouse and it backed into one of the open roll-up doors. It was almost fully dark and I knew that I wasn't as making as much noise as I thought. With the idling diesel and the noise of the roll-up door, their ears would probably be ringing a little bit in the now-silent world.

I tried to look at the warehouse without silhouetting myself in the semi's headlights. Lanterns had been hung or placed on the ground near the back of the truck, and people were getting in and out unloading things. I couldn't tell what it was, other than the fact that it was a lot of boxes and large paper sacks.

The quiet murmur of voices told me that there were quite a few people there, and I debated going in guns-a-blazing, but in the darkness, I wouldn't know who was friend or foe. I didn't know what they'd done with the women and the children, so to do that, I could end up walking in and firing on innocents. No, I needed to be sure of my targets.

I had to move closer. Then, I heard the crunch of boot steps coming up towards me. I looked to my left just as a figure stepped in front of the headlights of the semi truck and walked directly towards me.

His face looked… No, it wasn't messed up, and he wasn't wearing a mask per se, but as soon as he stepped into the headlights, he pushed the mask up so the NVGs wouldn't blind him.

"Who are you and what you doing here?" a man's voice growled with a slight Russian accent.

I considered using my .22, but it wasn't suppressed. It might be loud enough to be heard over the thrumming sound of the semi truck. Pretend I was one of the boys.

"Hey man, I'm Larry. I just came in to see if I could check out the merchandise."

"Who are you with? You're not one of ours."

"I'm with the crew at the Museum," I lied. "Like I said, I'm just here to inspect the merchandise. We've got fifteen this time, so I want to make sure we're not getting cheated."

He moved closer, his gun up on me in an easy position. I tried to play it cool like I was used to having somebody point an automatic carbine at me. It looked like an H&K MP5, and with the calm confidence I could read in the man's eyes, he wasn't an amateur.

"Step back to the wall," he said. "Keep your hands up where I can see them."

He turned his head to the right to talk into a mic in the same instant that he stepped out of the semi's lights. My old training kicked in and when he was close enough to me, before he spoke, I closed the last few feet separating us. He was half a heartbeat away from pulling the trigger when my fist connected with his windpipe. I slapped at the H&K with my left hand, expecting gunfire that would bring everybody running, but the man slowly dropped to his knees, clutching at his throat and making gagging sounds.

The H&K was on a drop sling like mine, but he was more worried about getting a breath in. It was unfortunate, only a trach would save him. I finished him off with a vicious twist and dragged his corpse further into the gloom. I wanted to strip his corpse of everything useful and valuable, it had almost become the standard, but I needed to move. I grabbed the NVG's off his head and tucked them into the backpack I carried, and pulled some loose trash that was filling up the doorway of an adjacent building over him. If I had time, I would come back for the gun and supplies, but things were about to get busy.

A sudden revving of the semi's motor had me turning. I hadn't been in the light, but the man I'd killed had. Was this part of a normal patrol? If the truck pulled out the same way it had pulled in, I would be exposed… I had a half a second to decide and I grabbed a loose piece of cardboard and jumped down next to the corpse. The semi revved again and lurched forward, shifting gears as it slowly rolled out. The shouts from the warehouse behind it almost sounded like they were yelling 'good luck', but I couldn't be sure. My blood was pumping too hard and my own heartbeat was deafening to me.

Lights washed over my hiding spot, blinding me and making me lose my night vision, and then they were gone. I tried to take a breath, but the anxiety and adrenaline had me so high and so jacked up that I couldn't for a moment or two. I finally drew in a gasping breath, having held it previously without thinking about it, and I listened as the roll-up door closed. I sat there, waiting next to the cooling corpse of the man, before deciding to get the NVGs out and use them for what they were intended.

I pulled them back out of my pack and put them on. I noted they were third-generation Russian military surplus, something I'd used when I'd needed to use sanitized gear in the past. I turned them on and the night flickered to life with a green glow. The dim sources of light in the warehouse windows shone brightly, but it was the outside of the warehouse that I wanted to check out before I moved.

"Sergei," a voice crackled nearby, in the same accent.

I didn't quite jump out of my own skin, but it was a close thing. It had sounded loud, but then again, everything did. The voice crackled again, sounding like a bad radio, "Sergei, you taking a shit again?"

It was an earwig. I was so close to the corpse I could make it out. I rolled the corpse on its back, leaned over the left shoulder and touched the mic button.

"Nyet," I said, hoping to buy some time.

"Get your ass in gear, you didn't make the south corner checkpoint and I have to piss."

"Da," I agreed and then got up.

At least, I had an idea of where the next guy was going to be. Instead of avoiding the area, I pulled out my knife, holding it against the inside of my forearm and got up. In the daylight, nobody would confuse my Keltec KSG for an H&K MP5, but I was roughly the same size and build as the man I'd killed and both of our guns were on drop slings. Sure, I was heavier armed, but I didn't plan on him seeing me or if he did, for only as long as it took to take him out silently.

I started walking the same direction Sergei had been heading and checked my surroundings. Nothing. I would make the circuit of the building and walk as bold as brass up to his partner and…

Kill him? Knock him out? Question him? I was pretty sure I was going with the first, but I was letting my instincts guide me. I'd had enough training and experience, if I could keep my head straight. The thing that was niggling in the back of my brain was the accent and the name. The guy was obviously either a Russian immigrant or one of the many men who'd grown up in a home of immigrants… or… maybe he was from Russia? The voice on the other end had the same accent, both of them with a little bit of a Moscow sound to them. I decided they must be immigrants and wracked my brain.

A thousand years ago I'd been fluent in many languages, but I'd not used them in so long. I wasn't able to mimic accents back then, so I never even tried. Still, the guys were talking English and it was just one of a thousand thoughts that were running through my head as I turned the last corner to see a man standing there, the glow of him taking a big drag on a cigarette, bright in the NVGs.

"Jesus," he said, looking up at the sound of my footfalls, "I thought I was going to piss myself."

He never saw the knife until he was holding the scarlet line that had been drawn across his throat. I eased the body down, letting the cigarette fall from his mouth into the growing pool of blood and kept him from thrashing and making a lot of noise, and his hands away from any weapons.

"Sorry, friend," I told him. "Just checking out the warehouse."

I patted his pockets and found a set of keys. I took them and stuffed them in my pocket and walked towards the side door he'd been waiting near. I checked it and it was unlocked. I pushed it open slowly, just enough to look in. I saw outlines of people moving and unloading boxes from pallets and loading up a pickup truck. The lights from the lanterns inside were bright, almost blinding to me, so I turned off the NVGs and pushed them up on my forehead and slid inside, closing the door.

It took me at least a good minute to get my eyes adjusted, and I could see it was a truck similar to the body shape of the one I'd taken and had Jamie stash down the road. I smiled and looked around a bit. I could hear soft snores from one end, but most of the warehouse was bathed in a deep dark gloom.

Unless the moonlight or a lantern was casting a glow, I was going to have to use the NVGs to see.

I made my way towards the men working, using the deep shadows. Even though the lantern's light was almost blindingly bright to me in the NVGs, the men's night blindness would be worse than mine. I chanced a look over my shoulder and saw at least two dozen men sleeping on the floor. This was a staging area, I realized. It might not even be the main group. Despite that, there were pallets and pallets of bags and boxes. I couldn't make them all out, but they looked like the burlap style feed bags you'd buy from the feed store for…

Then it hit me. This was their food drop. Their main location, where they divvied up things. I would have to do what I'd come here to do and get out.

"Hey man," I heard someone yell.

I thought they were talking to me so I spun, but one of the men who was stacking boxes and bags into the truck turned to answer.

"Yeah?" he asked, his accent all Chicago with not a hint of foreign in it.

"Get on the horn and get Sergei and Dimitri in here to help us unload, would ya? I hear the museum group got a bunch of new broads for us to break in before we send them out on the ship. I don't want to wait, ya know?"

I could make out the man's smile despite the distance and the NVGs' dislike of the light he was holding. "Yeah, that sounds like a good idea."

"Those two schmucks helping us, we'll get this

done quicker… and we can wake Manny's ass up to go make the drop."

"On it," he said, holding up a finger and getting a radio off his belt.

I don't know why it hadn't occurred to me before, but the guys had working coms as well as NVGs, whereas the rest of the electronics around here were all fried. I had even used the NVGs without thinking about it, just taken it as a matter of fact. This gear was either hardened, which I doubted, or it had come from somewhere else. I listened as he tried calling for the men and chanced a glance back to where the sleeping men were. No movement.

I pulled a grenade out of a pouch, pulled the pin and threw it as hard and as far as I could. I couldn't track it in the blackness where the sleepers were, but I knew I'd overthrown them. Exactly what I'd wanted to do. I crouched right after the throw, next to a 55-gallon drum of something. The explosion came within heartbeats of it hitting and the screams of surprise, terror and pain filled the room. The men who were loading the truck waited half a heartbeat and then started rushing towards the commotion.

I pulled on the chain to roll up the doors and I got it up about five feet high before one of the men running noticed something. I don't know if it had been a draft of fresh air or the moonlight… but he turned and saw me silhouetted in the opening doorway. I waited until he spun, then pulled the KSG up and shot him in the chest. The flash of the gun was bright and overloaded them for half a second, but I was already running. I had just enough room to clear the top of the truck in the doorway, I hoped.

Screams and shouts met me, and I pushed the NVGs up and pulled the pin of another grenade and threw it towards the loudest of the screams. It went off and for a moment, I could see the three figures that had been thrown from their feet. I felt the wind brush my cheek and then the sharp deafening crack of a bullet going past my head, so I rolled and came up in front of the truck. The semi had come in the left door, and the truck was in the central door that I'd opened, so I was pretty much screwed as gunfire erupted around me. I had more grenades, but I needed to not kill everyone. Still, gunfire pinged off the concrete floor every time I tried to poke my head out.

Instead of going around, I hit the ground on my stomach and looked under. I could see men rolling on the ground and with a start, I realized that I'd shut out all sound. I listened harder, trying to pick out everything.

"He's in front. You two take the right, I'm on the left and we'll..."

"No way, my brother needs the medic, I have to—"

"Don't fucking argue," the man who was out of sight said. "Now, you ready?"

"Fucking dumb-ass mafia motherfuckers!" somebody behind them screamed. "Let him get me to the medic!"

I pulled the pin on the grenade and prayed. I didn't throw it, I slid it under the truck. For a horrifying moment, it slid off the passenger side rear tire on the undercarriage, but then it bounced off the side like a pinball. I closed my eyes, and when the explosion rocked the night, I was already on my feet with the shotgun primed and ready. One man was on his feet and I got a snapshot off as he was taking aim at me. It hit him in his gun arm and he dropped the H&K he'd been holding. I almost ripped the driver's side door off the truck when I got in.

I felt for the ignition, figuring that's where the keys were… because I needed to get this heap moving before they filled it – and me – full of holes. No keys… I flipped down the visor… No keys…. In desperation, I pulled at the keys in my pocket. They hung up, and I yanked. My pocket tore as they came out and I frantically looked for anything that looked like an ignition key. Surely they had more than one set for everything, right? Right?!

I jammed the first key in the ignition and the truck fired up. I ducked as the window behind me exploded and shards of glass sprayed inside the truck. I put the pedal down and let off the clutch, tearing out of there like my ass was on fire and my hair was catching. I felt several impacts from what had to be bullets hitting the bed, but nothing came through the cab.

They ran after the truck, shooting and I screamed out the back window, "The price for the broads just went up!"

CHAPTER 15

I drove most of the way towards the museum with the NVGs on before I slowed down enough to turn on the headlights and stow the goggles in my backpack. I had no idea if I was going in over-armed, but I wanted to be better safe than sorry. The way those guys had been armed, I should fit in… though I didn't realize if I even knew how many guys made the drops. Ooops. Still… I was driving their truck.

I made sure to drive slow as I neared the museum and hit the horn twice when I was a hundred yards away. Four men snapped awake and bolted to their feet. The guards had been halfway resting or napping and two of them rushed inside, while the other two held their hands over their eyes and stared at my headlights coming out of the gloom. I pulled up out front, next to their truck and killed the motor, leaving the headlights on.

"Hey, man. You lost?" one of the uptown boys asked me, walking my way with a pistol in his hand.

He was clean-shaven as was his partner, who was staying further back towards the museum's entrance.

"No, making a delivery," I said stepping out and holding my hands up.

I didn't know who he thought I was, but he lowered his gun.

"We weren't expecting you until the morning, and this is only half of it."

That's what I was counting on.

"Yeah, well you know how Manny is when there's new broads to be had," I said with a fake grin, wanting to throw up at the words.

"Yeah, that horny bastard can hardly wait. I think he jacks off every time he comes to do a pickup," he said laughing. "I'm scared to even use the bathroom after him."

"Speaking of that, man..." I said, making a pained expression, lit by the afterglow of the headlights and I nodded my head towards the museum. "Can I use yours?"

"Man, I don't know about that. The working toilet is upstairs by the girls, now that the middle ones are fucked, and the boss is a little jumpy."

"Tell you what," I said digging into my pocket. "Two .38 shells for the bathroom and a roll of toilet paper?"

The man smirked and his partner laughed out

loud.

"Three shells and you can have this," he said, pulling out a folded wad of paper.

If lucky, it was maybe a quarter roll of paper, but it had showed me how dedicated the guys were to the gang. Just like that, I'd trumped their security by bribing them.

"Where's the other truck?" the man asked, me swiping the shells and handing me the wad.

"It's coming soon. Can one of you make sure the girls are ready to move when we get one of these unloaded? I really gotta go."

"Yeah, buddy. Joe will do that," he made a dismissive gesture at me and looked at the building.

"Elevator work?" I asked.

"Better hold your cheeks, man," he grinned and walked to the back to inspect the bags.

I almost took off at a run but kept a pained expression on my face and the TP in my hand. Joe, the man who'd stayed at the steps, grinned at me and nodded before walking down to join the first guard. I walked in and a few men were lounging around by a desk, but none of them looked up in alarm.

"You here to do the pickup?" one of them asked.

"Yeah, but I gotta use the…" I held up the flattened roll of TP.

"Oh yeah, top floor, use the stairs. First right. The ladies room still works. If one of the dumb cunts is in there, boot her ass out. Bunch of crybabies, this bunch is."

"Got it," I said.

I rushed the staircase to find a half-awake man

in front of the doorway with a deer rifle held loosely in his hands. He was wearing tattered jeans and a flannel shirt, with his dark hair poking up in the back. Mentally, I named him Alfalfa.

"I heard you guys were here. Some of the girls are in the shitter before we send them out. You want me to..."

"Man, I don't have time to wait," I said, pushing my way in.

"Heh, I've had days like that," he said laughing. "Hope it all comes out ok for ya," he said and busted up laughing like it was the funniest shit he'd ever heard.

I just waved my hand backward and pushed my way in.

Two of the women were sitting there, with several in stalls crying.

"Oh God, please?!" A young blonde woman who was wearing the stained remains of white capris and a black bra wailed, "I've already had a turn tonight and I'm sore."

Her pleas were met and agreed on and somebody in the stall sobbed louder.

"Shut up, bitch," I roared.

They all flinched and I walked up to the one who'd spoken to me and got close. I heard stall doors cracking open and I pulled my .22 out of my waistband and held it out to the woman.

"Listen," I said softly. "I'm one of the good guys, and I'm sorry I scared you. In a couple of minutes, maybe ten, there's going to be a lot of gunfire. I'm here to get you out," I said, pushing the gun at her, handle first.

She shrank away, but a woman in her mid-thirties with dark hair and no clothing other than a pair of panties walked up and took the gun. I tried not to stare at her near nude form, but she had burn marks from what had to have been cigarettes, and bruising up and down the side of her body where she'd been beaten. Her black or brown hair had been chopped with what looked like a knife, and the lantern in the bathroom did little to hide the badly healed scar that ran down the side of her right cheek. She held the gun up at eye level with me.

"Say that again," she said.

I could have taken the gun, but I had given it to them as a sign of trust. Also, it was the only one without a round in the chamber. Wile E Coyote… super genius.

"I've set these guys up. There's going to be a gunfight and soon. When the men up here rush down to reinforce the men outside, we can all escape," I said trying not to talk too loudly, but the crying had stopped and two more women joined the group that was standing before me.

"You're a liar," the woman with my gun said, her breasts rising and falling as her breathing quickened in a fight or flight response.

"No, I'm not. I'm truly sorry that I didn't come back here sooner. I knew about these guys and—"

"You're the Devil Dog," Mary said, stepping in front of me.

My heart caught. Her long red hair was matted and she had a large bruise that covered half of her face. She wore a man's button up shirt and was trying to pull it closed to hide her nude form underneath it.

"I'm..."

"Hey, don't be like Manny," the guard outside the door said laughing. "Or if you are, let me know and I'll join you."

"I'm good, almost done," I shouted.

"Who's the devil dog?" the woman said, closing the distance so the pistol was almost touching my eyeball.

I hesitated. That was me, but Mary said... I blinked. It wasn't my ex-wife Mary, though it looked a lot like her. Dammit, I didn't need this. I had to be frosty and... the click of the gun hitting an empty chamber surprised me. She tried pulling it again and then started fumbling with it. I grabbed it out of her hands and stepped back, wracking the slide and putting my hands up.

"The Devil Dog is the dude who keeps hitting the gangs. He steals the girls and kids," the blonde woman said.

"Yeah, he sets them free," the redhead said.

"Is that so?" the one woman asked, the one who'd had the gun before - the one who'd just tried to kill me.

She advanced and I could see the fire in her eyes. The anger, the hatred, the humiliation. Despite my having a ton of gear and guns, she was in full beast mode and I had to put her at ease and diffuse the situation.

"Yeah, I'm here to help. If you ladies don't want

it, I'm going to leave when the shooting starts. Just… go tell the rest to be ready to move."

The woman's eyes flickered with something I couldn't make out in the dim light and she let out a big shuddering breath and her arms and hands started to shake.

"Oh god, you're for real," she said.

"Yes," I admitted. "I am. I need you to get the others ready to go. I expect them to come at any time."

"Who to come?" the redhead asked, letting go of the front of the shirt and stepping close to me.

"The men they were selling you to. They aren't coming for a pickup this time…"

"How do we get out? The stairs are covered," the blond asked.

"Who's going to carry the kids?" another asked.

"Somebody go and get them ready," I said, putting the .22 on safety and then handing the bold woman the gun. "Give that to somebody who can hide it," I told her. "Just in case. Safety's on. You all are stuck at the end of the hallway on the right?"

"Yeah," she said, handing the gun to the woman with the capris who stuffed it into a pocket. "Just make sure you aren't lying to me."

The fire was back in her eyes and I nodded. They grabbed the lantern and left, some sobbing. With fear or relief, I didn't know.

* * *

"You ok in there?" a voice called out.

"I think I had a bad burrito," I called from within the stall.

I wasn't sitting, but I had my knife out again. The blood from earlier had dried to a crust on some areas, and I could smell it. I was usually more careful about it, but I was winging this plan. Something my former superiors would have been horrified by.

"Ok, boss just said to check on you. We got most of the truck unloaded, so it'll be time to move the girls when the second truck comes."

"Oh yeah," I said in the gloom. "I know Manny was excited about this shipment," I said holding the knife out in case he came into the pitch black bathroom.

"I hear ya there. He wouldn't be sitting and shitting if he was here, he'd have one of those ladies bent over the…"

I hit the flush button and the swirling water surprised me. I hadn't seen any buckets up here for them to fill the old fashioned toilets, but somebody had apparently or they had running water.

"Yeah yeah," I said, "I'm coming—"

A staccato burst of gunfire shattered the night's silence and somebody from below shouted an alarm.

"Shit," the guard muttered and the door slammed shut.

I could hear running feet and I waited thirty seconds before I heard shouts and calls for reinforcement and gunfire from within and outside the museum. Time for me to exit stage left.

The lanterns on the top floor were bright to

my eyes at first glance, like coming out of my tunnels and into the daylight. I squinted and moved. I headed towards the women and saw two men rushing towards the stairwell behind me. I let them run past before turning and firing three shots off from the KSG. They fell, shot in the back right between the shoulder blades. They slumped to the floor, one of them not quite DOA. I put one more shot into him and then started walking, pulling shells from my right coat pocket and fumbling them into the odd spot in the back of the gun.

I was careful to get four shells, two into each loading tube, when I caught sight of another man poking his head around to see who was coming. He was the one who was guarding the ladies.

"What's going on?" I screamed to him, his eyes the only thing visible.

"They're shooting at us," he said. "The guys unloading the truck got gunned down. What the fuck are you guys doing?" he asked, a barrel of his rifle poking up around the corner.

He hadn't seen the bodies yet, but he'd heard the nearby shots. I'd been truly hoping that they hadn't left somebody to guard the women when the shooting started, but I'd never done something exactly like this. Every time I'd set out to try to save innocents and kill bad guys before, I'd had a rough plan and then made shit up on the fly when things went south, which they usually did.

"That isn't my guys! Manny and one other guy were bringing the other truck," I said, still holding the KSG at the forward position.

His eyes suddenly got wide and I could tell he was looking over my shoulder, taking in the still forms on the staircase, and then he moved. The rifle barrel I could see started moving down and he stepped around the corner. It was almost in slow motion as I raised the shotgun and let loose. The slug hit the corner of the wall next to the man's head and he flinched back, the gun going off despite me being ready and faster on the draw. A sickening pain and a sledgehammer blow hit my left side under the ribs and I fell to my knees as his bullet passed through me. Sometimes, Murphy played for the wrong team and tonight, he did.

Pop pop pop pop pop pop pop pop

I was holding a hand over my side when the blonde stepped out, a smoking .22 in her hand, holding the hand of a young girl no more than twelve years old.

"Oh shit!" she screamed. "He's shot!"

I was blacking out, not from blood loss, but from the pain. I felt hands checking me and something pressed on the wound, making me scream.

"How are we getting out of here?" the fierce woman said, filling my vision, a crazed look lit her face, making her seem like a woman out of the things nightmares are made of.

"I have a truck stashed half a mile from here. Help me up," I said, the pain bringing me back from almost passing out.

"How bad is it?" she asked, pulling on my good arm.

"I don't know," I gasped in pain as the crew from

the bathroom helped me to my feet, and women and kids came out of the room they'd been held in.

"Martha," the fierce woman said. "Lead us down the staff stairs, so I can help him move. Steffy, you get his other arm."

"But..."

"Move, woman!" she shouted.

"My .45," I said and Mary - wait it wasn't Mary. dammit! - the redhead nodded and reached in carefully and pulled the pistol out of the holster. "Yeah, that one's loaded. Just turn off the safety."

"What about those," she said, looking at my shotgun.

"If I can't use it, I'll let you know," I told her, my mouth going dry.

We made our way to the back, where a dented steel door was set into the wall. The staircase was old and probably part of the original construction of the museum. It was cramped, dark, and when my feet tried to trip me up, several hands got me by the back of the belt as we moved as one down the blackened stairs.

"Where's the truck?" the fierce woman asked me.

With a start, I realized that even though I was moving, I had spaced out. It was like the time I'd taken shrapnel when a landmine converted into an IED had gone off, seven years ago. They had been picking metal and concrete out of me for a few days. I'd walked to the medic before collapsing, not remembering the walk at all, made with the help of the men I'd served with.

"It's down there," I said, pointing to an abandoned paint store half a mile away, a little disoriented before I remembered the layout. We'd come out the west doors and I looked over my shoulder.

The west entrance had been barricaded from the inside, but we'd gotten through it without them noticing us. Gunfire still rang out… actually, it hadn't stopped but had picked up during our mad dash in the dark. Now, it was falling silent as voices, one by one that were screaming, fell silent.

"Where we going, where is it?" the redhead asked.

"The Sherman Williams on the right," I told her. "If you prop me in, I can drive us to the next stop where we've got people waiting for us."

* * *

The truck wasn't actually inside the paint store but parked beside it. We didn't have far to go, but I'd known that some of the ladies and kids could be in rough shape and I'd needed a way to move them quickly before the two gangs realized what I had done. The fierce woman had argued with me about driving, but only one other person knew how to drive a stick, and she was half comatose in shock from the rape and abuse she had suffered. So it was me.

"…and pinch those wires together. Don't touch them cuz they will spark…" I was telling her.

There were three ladies and myself in the truck. Bodies upon bodies were packed inside and out of the truck, making the tires almost rub against the bed's wheel wells.

"Shit," she hissed, but the starting wire had been held on long enough and I pumped the gas pedal and the truck fired up.

It ran rough for a moment, but it smoothed out quickly.

"Turn on the lights," the bossy one told me.

"Get the goggles out of my backpack and put them on me," I told her.

I could have done it, but that would've made me twist, and I couldn't twist. I'd given her my pack, so I could sit in the seat properly and the only thing I still had was the KSG, which was pinched between the women and me. She swore and a second later I felt the goggles being awkwardly placed on my head.

I reached up and adjusted them, flipped them on and lowered them. I put the truck into gear and headed out slowly, trying not to hit high RPMs, which would have echoed. Maybe not enough to overpower the gunfire, but in a dead city, motors were a rare thing to hear and the sound carried far.

"Watch out," the fierce woman said, pushing the wheel to the left.

"I got it," I said with a start and realized I had been passing out.

I wiggled and a bolt of pain went through my body. I could feel both my stomach and back sticking to the shirt, pulling at the wound. There was an old hotel ahead of us, where I had planned on meeting everyone in the sub-basement. Instead,

I felt myself drifting. My eyes closed again and I heard screams. Startled, I opened them and pulled the wheel sharply as metal on metal screeches could be heard from me glancing off the side of a truck.

"You're passing out," she said. "Stop the truck before someone back there gets killed."

She was right, and the women in the back would be having a rougher time than us inside. I came to a stop and felt for the mass of wires with my right hand. My arm brushed the fierce woman's leg and she shot me a look, but I pulled the wires loose to kill the motor.

"Yeah, we're basically here," I said, my mouth and lips dry.

I felt on my belt for my water bottle. I'd always carried two quarts when in the sandbox, and I was parched. I could always get more water from a supply truck further back in the convoy. I cracked open my door, waiting for the soldiers behind me to back me up, and I reached for the water bottle to find the cold metal and plastic of the KSG that swung at my side. Right. I wasn't in Afghanistan. Got it. Understood, sir, I…

I was falling again. I heard shouting, and as I hit the ground, tilting everything ninety degrees, I saw three figures running towards the truck, two of them women, one a young man. I thought it—

CHAPTER 16

"H*old him still,*" I swear that's what I thought I heard.

I felt a straw placed in my mouth and I sipped. Sweet nectar of the Gods, it was good! I tried to get more, but the straw was removed. I was tired, sleepy, warm. I felt a pinch on my arm and then a growing numbness. I half dreamed, half felt hands working on me. Another pinch, this time on my side. Pills were pushed into my mouth. I tried to spit them out, but gentle hands pushed them back against my lips and the straw was put back.

I swallowed just to get another sip of whatever it was in the cup, washing the nasty flavor away. I slept.

* * *

I felt more pinching, hands examining me. My side was pins and needles of pain and pleasure. Somebody pulled me onto the side I hadn't been shot in recently and I could feel the same sensation on my back as several sets of hands held me up.

"I don't know," I heard Salina's voice say. "He's lost a lot of blood…"

* * *

"Can you brush my hair?" Mouse's voice cut through my sleep-addled brain.

Pain wracked my body. My side was sore and everything around the gunshot felt hot and stiff. I tried to crack open an eyelid, but it was like they were glued shut. My mouth was as dry as the sands of the desert I had been dreaming about and I could taste the blood on my cracked lips. I had been out for a little while, maybe days. I worked at it and I was able to get one exhausted eye to finally open. Excruciating pain hammered me from the bright assault on my eyes. It took me a moment to get my focus and Mouse was sitting there with a pouty expression. She had a silver brush with an ivory handle, her favorite brush, in her outstretched hand.

"Hold on, little dormouse," I told her. "I'm not feeling so hot…"

I realized that I wasn't in the tunnels. That more than anything else got my other eye open and I could see sunlight streaming into what looked like a surgical theater, except… there were windows and I could see the sun reflecting off of the glass of a building across the street. We were topside somewhere… and Mouse was here with me…

I tried to get up, but a wave of nausea washed over me.

"Momma Salina!" Mouse screamed and ran for the door, "Uncle Dick is awake!"

I heard footsteps… like a herd of elephants, to be honest, and I was pushing myself as much as I could to sit up, but it wasn't happening. There was too much pain and I was too weak. I collapsed in curses and sweat from just that little bit of exertion and waited.

Jamie, Mel, Danielle, Jeremy, Salina, and the fierce woman stalked in. All were wearing clean clothing and had recently washed. The bruising on the fierce woman was almost completely gone and I knew I had to ask her what her name was, so I could quit picturing her standing in that bathroom, mostly bare and ready to kill me… Hell, she had pulled the trigger on me.

"Dick, are you..." "Don't crowd him, let me through." "I told you I should have gone with you." "You got them all back." Their words washed over me, but it was the silent woman, the dark haired, fierce one, who never said a word that caught my attention.

"Stop!" Salina yelled. "Let me talk to him. You all get out!" Her voice was deafening, and although my body had recognized that I was dehydrated and had somewhat of a headache, that sent a bolt of pain through my skull.

I winced and they all turned to go.

"You too, Miss," Jerome said from the doorway to the fierce woman.

"No," she said simply, walking to the corner and propping herself there as if daring the big man to come and move her.

"Who are you?" I asked her.

"Courtney," she said, warily watching me.

Salina gave her the stink eye and when Jerome started in the room towards her, Salina put up a placating hand to stop her son.

"Where am I, this isn't the clinic?" I asked.

"Emergency Veterinary Hospital," she said. "Though I had the bed brought in from the clinic."

I nodded.

"How bad am I?" I asked Salina.

"You're too stupid to die, you know that? I ain't never seen a man as dumb as you. I figure you'll still be alive in a month, if you don't die from infection. Longer than a month, if you quit running into every gunfight in the city."

"When you get tired of patching me up, just say the word, Doc," I said grinning.

Her annoyance and insults were something I'd suffered before. She didn't mean it, it just meant that I'd scared her and this was her way of showing it. I couldn't really blame her.

"Oh, I will. Now shut up and let me check you out."

She did and then peeled back the bandages. I tried not to cry out in pain, but I did wince. The gunshot had gone through and through as I had thought.

"Don't be a baby," Salina said. "Otherwise, your flinching is going to make me miss, and I have to make sure the wounds don't start seeping any worse than they are."

"Didn't you stitch me closed, Doc?" I asked her, trying to see how bad it was.

My side was a rainbow of hues ranging from green, yellow and dark purple from bruising. The flesh around the gunshot was puckered and red. I didn't have the telltale signs of infection, though.

"No, we're letting it seep. You're going to have to keep this packed and change the bandages frequently."

I winced in more than just pain. It was at how much it was going to cost in the way of materials, supplies and ammunition. We needed everything we had and…

"What are you such a sourpuss about?" Courtney said.

My eyes shot to her. For a while, I had forgotten she was in the room. She walked closer to me, with Jerome watching silently from the doorway.

"How much is this going to cost me, Doc?" I asked her.

"After tonight, I think all debts are paid," she said, her smile and the Caribbean lilt of her voice putting me at ease.

It wouldn't be all that horrible… wait, all debts paid?

"Excuse me?" I asked when the implications of her words hit me like a ton of bricks. "What do you mean, after tonight?"

"Oh, yeah... We explained it to you the other day, but I don't know if you remembered or not. You were pretty in and out of it," Courtney said.

"Where's Maggie?" I asked her, desperate to know where my daughter was suddenly.

Salina and Courtney exchanged glances.

"Where's my daughter, is she ok?" I begged.

"Who are you talking about, Dick?" Salina asked. "Are you looking for Mouse or Melanie?"

Melanie. Mel. I blinked my eyes, and the irrational fear and pain that had been building up in my chest suddenly left me. I felt so tired, and I hurt all over.

"I... Sorry, I..."

Courtney stalked over to the bedside. I saw Jerome stiffen, but Salina just shifted her gaze and took a step to the side.

"Hey, they've been filling me in. You've been out of it for almost a week since you rescued us," she said. "You're sick and hurt and the last thing you need to do is to give the doc here even more sleepless nights. We'll find your daughter, but I need you to stay with us this time."

"This time?" I asked her, wanting to know so much more.

I'd been out for a week? I was obviously topside, but so were the others. If Mouse was topside, then Pauly was somewhere near, he never left her side. Then, there was the fact that both Danielle and Jeremy were up here. Nobody left the little kids alone, ever. Somebody always stayed behind. In fact, now that I was thinking about it, Mel and Jamie were topside here. Didn't they understand how dangerous it was? Didn't they...

"You've woken up twice now," Salina said. "You've seemed lucid and then you'd go back to sleep for a half a day. Then this past time, for two days. It's been roughly eight days since you were shot."

No wonder I felt dehydrated.

"Can I have some water?" I asked, and Jerome smiled for the first time since I'd woken up.

"He's good," he grinned and walked out of the room to return a minute later with a glass.

"Yeah, I think he's back with us this time," Salina said.

I knew I wasn't supposed to gulp, but they'd only given or forced just enough fluids in me to survive. I knew that with the blood loss, that had probably complicated things.

"I hope I'm back," I said, trying to pace myself. "I... I have to talk to Jeremy. Is everyone topside? What's been..."

"Rest. Drink some water. Don't drink too much too fast, but you need to hydrate. I'll be back with some hot broth soon. You need to drink all of it. Especially the broth."

"How close was I?" I asked her.

"Did you see the light?" Courtney asked me.

"What?" I asked her, my voice cracking and I turned my head to look at her.

"What is she talking about?" I asked Salina.

"I... Jerome, would you go check on the kids for me? I'll be fine in here."

"Yes, Momma," he said and pulled the door closed behind him, leaving me alone with both ladies.

"What's going on?" I asked Salina. "What are you talking about?" to Courtney.

My neck was tiring out from looking from one to the other, so I laid my head back and closed my eyes.

"You had lost so much blood. Your heart stopped and we were able to get it started again. We were lucky that I already had your blood type. You're the same blood type as Jerome and Courtney here. We had to rig a way to do a transfusion, but you'd lost so much blood that it took both of them…"

In another time, another world… the junkie part of me, the self-loathing part of me wouldn't care. The rational side of me immediately made me think of STDs and blood-borne pathogens. And in the end, I didn't care.

"Thanks for saving me," I said to both of them. "Is that why my whole chest hurts?" I asked her.

"You mean from the CPR?" she asked me.

"Well, yeah," I told her. "I feel like one big bruise."

"You were shot," Courtney said pointedly, "and you're welcome. I'm glad the gun wasn't loaded the first time."

Salina shot her a puzzled look, but Courtney shrugged and went back to her corner and leaned against the wall again. I took another long gulp of the water. My eyes widened a little bit when I realized it was a Slurpee cup, a remnant of my old life. I could almost remember the mind numbingly sweet flavor of a Slurpee… and then there was nothing else left in the glass.

"You know," I said holding it out to Salina. "There're two things… what do you mean all debts are paid off after tonight… I mean, my whole family is topside. What's up with that? And two, did anybody see you giving me CPR?"

Salina gave me a puzzled look and then told me.

"We brought you here first because it was closest. Jamie had to drive you and Mouse wouldn't leave your side the moment she heard you'd been hurt badly. Then, after the community attacked the warehouse and pushed the guys to the wharf—"

"What are you talking about?" I asked her, coughing.

"I forgot, you were still pretty out of it," she said. "Luis, Jeremy, and a dozen men you know from the market attacked the mafia guys, or gang or whatever they wanted to call themselves. The Russian mob?"

"Sounds about right," Courtney said.

"So, your plan to pit one against the other sort of worked. About two dozen came back, only to walk into an ambush. The guys that weren't cut down, fled to the wharf. There's a big ship out there, a container ship."

"I don't understand," I told her.

"Jeremy was half insane," the doc told me, "and when Luis and a bunch of other guys heard… well… Your words really hit home. They decided to do something about it."

"What words?" I asked her, still confused.

I mean, I apparently had died and been revived. I was on some sort of pain killers I was sure and definitely dehydrated. Still, what words?

"Apparently your boy was in some sort of fight," Courtney said answering, "and instead of killing the men involved, you berated them, beat one pretty bad, and busted another. Then, you paid for his treatment. You shamed them. You showed them what it meant to be a better human being."

"You don't even know me!" I said, suddenly angry, but not knowing why.

"I don't need to," she said. "I almost killed the most decent man alive, well, except for Jerome. He's pretty awesome," she gave Salina a grin. "You're all anybody's talking about right now."

I closed my eyes. I was used to being a loud, abrasive, ass. Especially in public and at the market. People wouldn't mess with me when they knew the junkyard dog was on the prowl and I had a family to keep after.

"So, they killed them and pushed the rest back into some sort of ship?" I asked the doc.

"Yes. We had a couple of small injuries on our side. We recovered a lot of gear from that warehouse, by the way. That's what I'd meant when I said after tonight, all debts are paid."

"Why tonight?" I asked her.

"That's when we finish cleaning it out. As it is, we have men with scoped rifles taking shots at anybody who comes out on the deck of that ship. They probably have enough food cached for a long time, but so do we, now. At least for until the world seems less crazy."

The gangs had been killed or pushed out of the territory. The women, as far as we knew had been freed, and there were supplies for everybody for a time. That was what I'd set out to do. It didn't explain why everyone was topside, but it made some sort of sense. I mean, they would definitely feel safer, now that they didn't have to worry about getting snatched, and if the community had come out in force and worked together, something they hadn't done until now… They'd put the fear of God into any and all. I just wished they would have come together sooner and not been as cowardly before…

"Your face just scrunched up," Courtney said. "What was it? The thought."

"Why do you care?" I asked her, feeling stronger with the fluids working in me.

"Maybe because I feel horrible about what I did!" she said, almost screaming.

"What did you do?" I asked her, feeling slow because I understood it right after saying it.

"I had your gun to your head and I pulled the trigger!"

"I knew it was empty," I told her. "You were scared." I was feeling weak and nauseated again, and very, very tired.

"Then why did you hand me a gun?"

"It was the only way to get you ladies to trust that I was there to help. You'd been through so much… If I gave you a gun, you'd feel like you were in control. As it was, the gun was what saved me when I was shot."

"You deliberately did that?" she asked. Her volume was down, but I could tell she was as pissed as I was.

"It sounds like he played a little psychology on you, girl," Salina said walking over and putting a calming hand on her arm. "And it worked."

"Yeah, well… shit… thank you," Courtney said and started for the door.

I laid there, my eyes tracking her. She paused at the door before turning, "I mean that, and I'm sorry… I'm sorry for pulling the trigger. At that moment, you were every man who'd…"

"Courtney," I rasped. "I don't blame you, but if it's forgiveness you need, you have it. I just wish I could have helped you sooner. I'm sorry it took me so long."

She made an exasperated sound and pushed open the door so hard it stuck open.

"What was that about?" I asked Salina, who'd walked over to the bed and taken my empty cup.

"She's waited a week to tell you that. I didn't know it went down quite like that, but…"

"It was bad. I feel horrible that it took me wanting to get back to my daughter to finally work to kill off those fuckwads. They were in bad shape, the abuse and the…"

"I know, Dick," she said, using her calming touch on me now. "I treated them, all of them. You did the best you could, but let me ask you something…"

"Go ahead."

"Do you think you're better than all of us?"

Her question caught me off guard. "No?!"

She looked at me then shook her head, "Why do you think you needed to do it? Why did it have to be you? Because you're better than us? Had more training? Why?"

The accusation in her words stung.

"Because I should have already. I was too scared to do it when I should have," I admitted.

"So were we."

Those words sort of clicked inside of me. Like a lightbulb moment you'd see in the old black and white cartoons when they had a good idea or enlightenment. Well, that was my enlightened moment, too.

"We should have all worked together before," Salina said. "But we weren't trusting. It took a beat up, shot up, grouchy old veteran to show us what we were like before. As little as we help each other out now, you showed us that even a junkyard dog like you had more compassion that we did. Don't be sorry for waiting so long. We're all guilty of that. We need to move forward."

"Ok," I said, putting a hand up as if to stop her.

God, I was so tired, my eyes wanted to close, but I was so damned thirsty, and my stomach was now rumbling so bad it was cramping. As much as I wanted to sleep, I knew that the hunger would keep me awake.

"You know," I said, looking her in the eyes by moving my head. "You never answered my second question."

"What was it again?" she asked.

"Did people see you giving me CPR?"

"Yes, half the community."

"So all the guys out there saw your lips on mine? They'll be so jealous of me!"

Her cheeks turned red and she sputtered for a second, "I think your chest is going to be fine, but I don't know how your neck supports that big fat head of yours."

"Oh my God," Mel said from the doorway. "Did he just crack a joke?"

"If you want to call that humor," Salina said, motioning for the girl to come in.

She held a steaming coffee mug and I could smell it. Broth? Bullion? Whatever it was, my stomach rumbled.

"It's too hot right now," Mel said. "You scared us, Dick."

"Sorry, kid," I told her, watching as she pulled out a straw from her pocket and set both the mug and straw on a rolling cart near the bed.

"When I get all patched up, we'll make plans for heading west," I told her.

"Good. Mom and I… we talked about going anyways…"

"Don't," I told her. "It's not safe."

"We're not going to," she said. "We're going to wait a bit. Some of what we found in the mob guy's supplies were radios. Working radios. We're picking up transmissions from Kentucky. Some dude named Blake. We're going to wait for you to heal up because it sounds like it isn't safe anywhere right now."

"The devil you know," I said, feeling so tired I could barely keep my eyes open.

The smell of the broth was the only thing keeping me up.

"Yeah, Mom said something like that… and I was—"

CHAPTER 17

There were a lot of days where I would just fall asleep due to exhaustion, and I did end up with an infection for a while. I was lucky they'd driven the gang out of the warehouse, though, because there'd been enough medicine there to keep Salina stocked up. Surprisingly, she hadn't had to use any narcotics on me except when she'd been performing the meatball surgery to save my life. I hadn't even known or felt it. The rest was good old ibuprofen. The pain made it hard to get about, and I was sore and stiff.

"How much longer can you two wait?" I asked Mel, who was sitting on the hood of a dead car.

It had been three weeks since I'd woken up. My wound had mostly closed up, mostly. It still hurt every day, and I had a feeling that it'd hurt on cold days, the same way my shrapnel scars always did.

"We're waiting for you to heal up," she told me, for probably the thousandth time.

"I'm getting antsy to go. I don't know how long I can wait," I told her.

"You know, Mouse is going to miss you."

"I'm going to miss all of them," I told her.

"I know, but most of the little ones found families. The rest are going to stay with Danielle and Jeremy topside. You were like Mouse's boogeyman catcher or something."

"Or something, Maggie," I told her smiling.

She gave me a look, not on purpose, but I realized I'd done it again.

"Was kidding," I lied.

"No, you weren't," Mel said. "Part of you is broken, just like a lot of us are. We're healing, Dick. You will, too."

I knew she was talking about more than the hole in my side and for what it's worth, I agreed. I was broken, but I felt good for once. I felt antsy and ready to tackle my demons if it meant I'd be one step closer to my daughter.

"I know, I just… It's embarrassing… and hard to talk about," I admitted.

"You've done more and been hurt more than most," Mel told me. "So maybe, it'll take you a little longer to heal."

"I think so," I admitted, feeling like I was sitting next to the world's most mature teenager.

She had that effect on me and maybe that was the reason why I'd gotten her confused with Maggie more than anyone else. She was how I pictured my daughter being in my mind. I'd been thinking about Maggie a lot lately. My memory was faulty to some extent, probably from the drugs and abuse I'd put my body through, but I remembered her in small patches, like a short video clip, or from pictures I'd seen. Still images. I could almost hear her voice, remember what she sounded like, but when I got close to the memory, it'd leave me.

"I wanted to talk to you about something else," Mel said.

"What's that?" I asked her.

"Well, Courtney and Luis are a thing now. You knew that, right?" she asked with a look about her that made me think she was expecting me to be angry.

"Yeah, for about two weeks now," I told her, watching the surprise light up her face and making its way to tug her lips up and into a smile.

"Oh, phew," she said, wiping at her forehead in an exaggerated motion. "Well, Courtney's got family down in Texas. She wants to come with us when we all go."

I thought about it and shrugged. I could use the help. Luis had become more than just security for the market, though losing him would hurt the community.

"Can the community afford for him to leave?" I asked, knowing that asking a fifteen-year-old such a deep question might give me an unexpected answer.

"I think with everyone starting to work together, they'll be fine. Danielle said that she and Jeremy are going to keep an eye on the spot in the tunnels, but most of them feel safe enough to come topside for now. It's still their secret go-to spot."

"Kind of like ninja turtles?" I asked her.

"Something like that," she grinned.

I'd missed out on so many sunrises and sunsets living underground that every day that I could, I tried to watch the day start or end. I was doing it now, and I smiled when I saw four figures making their way towards us. Salina was holding hands with Pauly and Mouse, with Jerome bringing up the rear. I smiled at them. Mouse looked happy, and part of me deep inside wanted to lose my man card, and for a second, a tear almost ran down the side of my cheek. For like a microsecond. Maybe it was just my imagination.

"Uncle Dick," Mouse said as she got closer. "Would you like to brush my hair?" she asked, holding out the silver brush.

I tried to talk, but the words wouldn't come. A frog had apparently jumped into my throat and I made a weird sound. I swallowed and took the brush, meeting Salina's gaze.

"You'll be leaving us soon. Mouse wanted to say her goodbyes."

"Come here," I told her, and she scurried up the bumper and plopped down into my lap.

I took the brush and began pulling it through her hair. Pauly grinned at me and tugged at Salina's arm. She kneeled down to listen as he whispered something to her.

"I'm going to miss you, Uncle Dick," Mouse said.

"I'm going to miss you too, kiddo," I told her, choking up.

"I want you to find the real Maggie. She deserves to have a daddy."

"You tell him," Salina told Pauly.

"I'm going to miss you too, but we all know you need Maggie in your life," he said after a second.

"Did she make you say that?" I asked him, realizing how adult his statement was.

"We talked yesterday. I didn't have all the right words. Even though she helped me, it's what I think. You going to be going soon, aren't you?"

"Yeah, buddy," I said. "I'm leaving pretty soon. I'm going to miss the both of you, too."

Mouse turned and pulled the brush out of my hand and slid down, a smile lighting up her features.

"When you find her, give her a big hug from me."

"I promise."

I pulled out a picture I'd carried with me halfway across the world. I'd never had the chance to give it back to Mike's family, but if I was going to be going back to Mary's parent's farm, I'd drop off the picture for Mike as well. Mouse walked back to Salina, who took her hand. I gave the picture one last glance and stowed it away again.

"I'll be here if you want to talk," she told me. "But I would wait another week, even though I know you won't."

"I'll be in touch, Doc," I told her.

I watched them leave and I felt the car shift as Mel inched closer and leaned in, resting her head on my shoulder.

"Are you ok, Dick?"

"I think I will be. Someday," I told her, and with a start, I realized I actually believed it.

"I do, too. I miss my dad," she told me.

"I'll get you to him. I promise, Mel."

She smiled at me. "You got it right this time."

Someday soon, I would walk down the dirt driveway in Arkansas and open the door to find my daughter inside. I'd find that missing part of my soul and if she'd let me, I'd be the father I should have been the first time. I would get it right.

–THE END–

ABOUT THE AUTHOR

Boyd Craven III was born and raised in Michigan, an avid outdoorsman who has always loved to read and write from a young age. When he isn't working outside on the farm, or chasing a household of kids, he's sitting in his Lazy Boy, typing away.

http://www.boydcraven.com/

Facebook: https://www.facebook.com/boydcraven3

Email: boyd3@live.com

You can find the rest of Boyd's books on Amazon:
www.amazon.com/-/e/B00BANIQLG

Made in the USA
Monee, IL
05 April 2021